RECURRENCE PLOT

(and Other Time Travel Tales)

House of Future Sciences Books
www.afrofuturistaffair.com

Recurrence Plot (and Other Time Travel Tales)

A flash fiction version of *The Convention* originally appeared in *neon V magazine Vol I. the continuum + black excellence issue,* Autumn/Winter 2012.

A flash fiction version of *The Family Circle* originally appeared in *the State of Black Science Fiction 2012, Possibilities Anthology*, edited by Alicia McCalla, October 2012.

Published by The Afrofuturist Affair/House of Future Sciences Books, **www.afrofuturistaffair.com**

ISBN: 978-0-9960050-0-5

Cover Image by Kiara Monae
Cover Design by Annie Mok
Edited by Valjeanne Jeffers

DEDICATED TO MY GRANDMOTHER, MY MOTHER, AND MY DAUGHTER.
DEDICATED TO ALL MOTHERS AND CHILDREN WHO COME BEFORE AND AFTER ME.

Contents

Contents

THE FAMILY CIRCLE

(Mia)

At the moment when an act has been accomplished, light seizes it and carries it into space at lightning speed. It is incorporated with a ray of light; becoming eternal, it is eternally transmitted into the infinite.
— Camille Flammarion

The small box was carved out of a dark wood the color of the sea sitting in a sliver of moonlight. It sat on top of her dresser, which was also a wooden box: this one dirt brown and shabby, with a drawer missing from the middle like a row of gapped teeth. A large, frameless oval-shaped mirror with beveled edges hung above the dresser, situated directly across from the tiny room's only window.

Mia had arranged the furniture that way purposely, so that she was always looking out the window, even when her back was to it. The lone window, however, only overlooked an abandoned, trash-strewn lot behind the apartment building— a grim reflection of how she saw her own life.

Mia stood in front of the mirror now, observing all that it dully reflected through its thin film of dust: herself, the window, her six-year-old daughter sitting on the bed coloring her a birthday card, the small box on the dresser. . . Particles of dust traveled on rays of light through the window, hitting the mirror, scattering the light, and creating a glare that obscured her face.

She picked up the small box, performing a ritual that she had performed an endless number of times over the years: turning it over in her hands a few times; tracing the letters carved in wood at the top, which read *Family Circle;* rubbing her pointer finger and thumb against the small metal clasp; flipping the clasp up, and then back down. But Mia would never lift the lid, never check its contents. As a result, she did not know what the small box held or why it had those words carved into its face.

The small box was a companion as familiar to her as the lines of her favorite song. From the day she lost her mother on her seventh birthday up until today, her twenty-first birthday, it had traveled with her from foster home to foster home, throughout shelters, and finally to her very own box: a government subsidized studio apartment in a housing project, at the shadowy edge of North Philadelphia.

The small box had been packed right along with her and her daughter's few belongings when they moved in from the transitional housing shelter last week. All she had inherited from her mother was her birth certificate, a few photos, and the small box.

Mia had never opened the box because the choice of whether to open it or not was the only thing she felt she ever really had control over.

Most of the time, events seemed to happen to her, as if someone had planned her entire life's course without consulting her on it. Decisions were made for her and about her, but never *by* her. She had even birthed a child at the age of fourteen, like her mother, and a week after her own birthday, like her mother, reinforcing her own inability to shift her family cycle.

Her foster mother at the time called her bulging round belly "a curse," and told her that her "little fast ass was only bringing another gonna-be teen mom in the world."

Despite being a curse, Mia's baby girl felt like nothing but light growing inside her young body. She named her "Khepri," a name she had seen on the *Capri Sun* juice-boxes, but spelled differently. Khepri was her little light, a ray of hope, and a reason for change.

At the end of the day, though, nothing had ever changed. She was right back in the same box she had come from, with the same box in front of her. She had failed her daughter, making Khepri repeat her childhood.

Perhaps it was Mia's own mother who had chosen this path for her, for *them*, on that fateful day fourteen years ago today. That was the day her innocence ended, like an imploded planet. Since then she had been suspended inside of an endless *now*, a tuneless universe where nothing changed.

Sometimes Mia imagined that she was actually the reflection in the mirror that she stood before right now, instead of the person standing before it. Powerless, trapped under the weight of its own gaze, only able to reflect her world, never able to change it. Today, on her twenty-first birthday, and the fourteenth anniversary of her mother's suicide, however, there would be a change. Today, there would be a choice. Today, she would give herself a gift.

At some point along the way, she decided that she would open the small box on her twenty-first birthday, which was the same age her mother had been when she took her own life.

With that thought, Mia winced painfully as the last memory of her mother flooded her, as it did every birthday, fresh and alive as the day it happened.

They were living out of a motel room at the time, a room not much unlike the one she stood in now—small and boxy, sparsely furnished. A few dressers, a TV, small refrigerator, Holy Bible, and their suitcases. Everything was brown in her memory, the same brown on the rug, on the walls, on the dresser, on the Bible.

The only pop of color in the memory was her birthday balloons. Green, red, blue, orange balloons with mismatched string ribbons, taunting her from their spot huddled up against the ceiling.

As she sat playing and coloring, she would look up every so often to see her mother standing in front of the mirror, brushing her hair back off her face, stroking her wrist, listening to slow tunes from the little brown radio on the table in the room, singing along, drinking something clear out of a bottle.

Sometimes her mother would catch her eye in the mirror and smile sadly. Mia had always known her mother's smile to be sad, so nothing clued her into that day's smile being any different. Maybe it was just an inch sadder than usual, if she really focused hard on the details of the memory.

Right before her mother walked into the bathroom, locked the door and slit her wrists deep with a little razor blade, she remembered her mother coming over to her, kneeling down, and kissing her hard on the forehead several times.

She had said nothing to her little girl before she did it. No suicide note in the envelope with her little girl's birthday card, before or after the *Love Mommy* signature. No note with her body, either. No explanation. No final words of guidance.

No, all her mother left of significance, of goodbye as a birthday gift that kept giving, was this box and memories. A box that she had felt too weak to open, and memories that followed her around like lost and weary souls, no matter how many times she moved, how many drugs she did, no matter how hard it was to feed herself and the little girl that she brought into this world. She was her *self* still a scarred and scared little girl.

A motherless child mother.

And, maybe Mia had made it all up in her mind, that there was some meaning in opening it today, or that she even had a choice, either way. Maybe even this, opening it on her twenty-first birthday, was somehow fated, too; part of the events set in motion by her mother's horrible act on that day. It was a conversation she'd had with herself a million times over the years. How could she ever know, either way, whether she was *meant* to open the box today or whether it was her choice, after all?

No way of ever, ever knowing.

Mia chose/sealed her fate and she opened it now.

Gleaming in the dark was a bracelet. She lifted it out with two fingers and inspected it. This was what she had carried with the box for fourteen years, to the day: a bracelet, unlike any she had ever seen. Perfectly circular, it was made of twelve gemstones linked around a copper band, each stone with a unique shape and bearing an engraved astrological sign.

The largest stone on the bracelet was a glimmering, oval-shaped piece light blue stone with a Pisces symbol. This charm stood out to her because her mother, born on March seventh, had been a Pisces. And she, born today, March fourteenth, was also a Pisces. Her mother had always talked to her about how special that was to her because she had an interest in astrology. She would read their horoscopes for fun out of the daily paper whenever she got a hold of it. Sometimes she would point out the constellations in the sky if they were visible.

Like her mother before her, she had given birth at the age of fourteen, one week after her own birthday. Mia's own daughter would turn seven years old, seven days from today, on March twenty-first. Khepri's birthday was the first day of spring and the first day of a new sign, Aries, the first sign of the zodiac.

Beneath the bracelet inside the box, was a card that listed the astrological sign and each stone and a set of instructions for using *The Family Circle*.

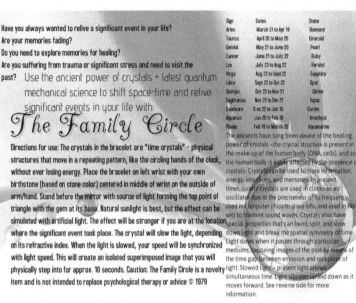

Have you always wanted to relive a significant event in your life?
Are your memories fading?
Do you need to explore memories for healing?
Are you suffering from trauma or significant stress and need to visit the past? Use the ancient power of crystals + latest quantum mechanical science to shift space-time and relive significant events in your life with:

The Family Circle

Sign	Dates	Stone
Aries	March 21 to Apr 19	Diamond
Taurus	April 20 to May 20	Emerald
Gemini	May 21 to June 20	Pearl
Cancer	June 21 to July 22	Ruby
Leo	July 23 to Aug 22	Peridot
Virgo	Aug 23 to Sept 22	Sapphire
Libra	Sept 23 to Oct 22	Opal
Scorpio	Oct 23 to Nov 21	Citrine
Sagittarius	Nov 22 to Dec 21	Topaz
Capricorn	Dec 22 to Jan 19	Garnet
Aquarius	Jan 20 to Feb 18	Amethyst
Pisces	Feb 19 to March 20	Aquamarine

Directions for use: The crystals in the bracelet are "time crystals" - physical structures that move in a repeating pattern, like the circling hands of the clock, without ever losing energy. Place the bracelet on left wrist with your own birthstone (based on stone color) centered in middle of wrist on the outside of arm/hand. Stand before the mirror with source of light forming the top point of triangle with the gem at its base. Natural sunlight is best, but the effect can be simulated with artificial light. The effect will be stronger if you are at the location where the significant event took place. The crystal will slow the light, depending on its refractive index. When the light is slowed, your speed will be synchronized with light speed. This will create an isolated superimposed image that you will physically step into for approx. 10 seconds. Caution: The Family Circle is a novelty item and is not intended to replace psychological therapy or advice © 1979

The ancients have long been aware of the healing power of crystals –the crystal structure is present in the make up of the human body (DNA, cells), and so the human body is easily affected by the presence of crystals. Crystals can be used to store information, energy, intentions, and memories. In present times, quartz crystals are used in clocks as an oscillator due to the preciseness of its frequency, used in computer chips to store info, and used in Radio sets to transmit sound waves. Crystals also have special properties that can bend, split, and slow down light and break the spatial symmetry of time. Light slows when it passes through particular mediums, capturing images of the past by means of the time gap between emission and reception of light. Slowed light + present light allows simultaneous time. Light vibrates up and down as it moves forward. See reverse side for more information.

After reading through the instructions quickly, she felt compelled to put the bracelet on, knowing it had belonged to her mother.

It felt so natural to slip the bracelet onto her left wrist, she hardly thought about it. But as soon as the cool band of bronze made contact with Mia's skin, it attached itself, warming up and becoming uncomfortably tight, squeezing so hard that her pulse throbbed.

Frightened by the sudden grip, she grabbed at the bracelet to pull it off. But it loosened just as quickly, the pain dissolving into a phantom lightness.

Just then, the light streaming through the window from the sun hit the Pisces stone, reflecting back into the mirror as Mia lifted her eyes from the bracelet on her wrist to look at her reflection. . . . and in that moment she could *see* herself clearly, her daughter playing on the bed behind her. The bracelet rested on her wrist comfortably now, because it was hers all along.

Back in my body, I remember. I glance up at the mirror and see myself clearly.

From the instructions on the card that came with the Family Circle, I know I will only have a few moments to be in this memory.

I spin away from the mirror to look at my daughter directly, who feels infinitely far away from me in the space between the dresser and the bed. It feels like I will not have enough time to reach her before the memory breaks, but I fight against the feeling, walking toward her, dragging light and matter and all of my regrets.

I finally make it over to my little girl. No sound will travel through this memory, so she will not hear me. Only light and image. I do not want to frighten her, but I must warn her. I kneel down to my daughter and kiss her on her forehead, mouthing the words, trying to impress them into her brain.

I love you. I am sorry. Break the circle. Don't open box.

The little girl does not understand what her mother is mouthing, but she will always remember the way each word feels as her mother pressed them into her forehead, the last kiss.

The little girl will always remember watching her mother walk back slowly to the dresser, take something off of it, and walk into the bathroom. She will always remember the sound of her fists pounding the door, after it seemed like her mommy stayed in there for a really long time.

The sound of silence after each time she called out to her mommy, said her name as many times as she could count (205). The little girl remembers going downstairs to the office her and mommy passed, with the guy she paid money to for them to stay there.

When she saw her mommy again several hours later, she was being taken out of the room on a bed with wheels, eyes big, not blinking or moving, staring at everything and nothing.

On the bathroom sink in the tiny one bedroom apartment in the projects, the police found a folded up, weathered advertisement for something called *The Family Circle*. On the back of the advertisement was an order form. Scribbled onto the lines of the order form was a note:

You may wish to further your studies of crystals for what they mat reveal of the mental, emotional, and physical states of your objects. For our guide on crystal studies, please use below order form and send $3.50 + $1.25 for S/H to: Future Sciences Bookshop PO Box 22333, Trenton NJ 08618

Name: I woke up again this morning knowing that I

Street Address: cannot leave this day. Yesterday. Today. Tomorrow is already the same. The days all melt into each other like disembodied memories struggling to

City: embody the present, ghosts

State: searching for   Zip: a body. These words are Notes: scripted, and I am simply tracing the lines. Tomorrow I will not wake up again.

_____
_____
_____
_____

RECURRENCE PLOT

(Khepri)

"It is easy to lose, through meddling or neglect, an entire aspect of existence. And sometimes, to cultivate a single new thought, you need not only silence but an entirely different life."
—Jennifer Moxley

<execute> Amenta Program </execute>

Read Forward.

PROLOGUE

As a child, before understanding that she experienced the world differently than others, her life, and the people in it, felt like the characters she would read about in the plays in her school textbooks at night, under her covers with a flashlight. Everything she heard and saw felt scripted. She knew what people would say before they said it. What people would do before they did it.

The phenomenon seemed to grip her soon after she turned seven and entered DHS, the foster care system in Philadelphia. Most children began to experience the onset of childhood amnesia around that age, where they can no longer recall past memories.

For the little girl, it was just the opposite— she could remember every event of her life with excruciating detail.

But it was not only past events that she could remember.

She could also remember *future* events and details in her life. It was almost like being able to rewind or fast forward a movie in her head and see scenes from that movie, or flip back and forth through the pages of a novel.

The little girl could look back and recall, in very specific detail, events from being born forward. She could, with the same detail, read ahead and see older versions of herself. The reason why she knew it was herself in older form was because she could not only see the events, but she was also *inside* her own head, hearing her thoughts. She could stand in front of a mirror of herself at any age, and peer out through the eyes of her own head.

Around the age of eleven, the little girl felt that she had finally acquired enough language and courage to explain to the lady she lived with at the time, Mrs. B, what was happening to her. She gave her very explicit details of things that had happened to her, and things that *would* happen to her in the future.

Mrs. B just dismissed these accounts until they became too frightening for her to deal with. Mrs. B reported it to the DHS worker, who then made her take the little girl to one of the free therapists at the drug rehabilitation center.

After a few appointments, the therapist told Mrs. B and the girl that he had researched a few similar cases and talked with some of his colleagues. He thought that the little girl might have something called: "paramnesia."

The psychologist said it was a confusion of fact and fiction, probably from a psychological trauma she had experienced as a young child, or perhaps from a head injury. Sometimes, he explained, paramnesia was experienced as a prolonged moment of *déjà vu:* the feeling of always having been there, in that moment. Believing that you knew what was to unfold as it unfolded. Combined with a bit of narcissism and imagination, it made the sufferer believe that he or she could "see" into the future.

But the little girl tried to explain to him, again and again, that she didn't just believe she knew what was going to happen. She *knew.* Everything in her world, everything she experienced, always happened the way it played out for her moments before.

The girl tried to explain that the scenes played out in her body, like she was moving a second faster than the speed of light and could catch what was going to happen or being said just a very small moment before it happened.

And she tried to explain how scary and lonely it was, to live that one moment before everyone else—to be weighed down constantly by the memory of every moment before—living life as one, long, perfect memory of the past and the future that you cannot escape from, bury, or leave behind.

The therapist told Mrs. B to start the little girl off with two pills a night after dinner for anxiety.

The little girl resisted the little round pills at first because they were so hard to swallow, and tasted chalky, and always got stuck in her throat. But after a week, she began to forget things. Outcomes became fuzzy, memories turned blurry and were no longer perfect.

But still she suffered.

When the little girl turned 14 years old, she finally found a way to make the memories go away for good, how to become stuck in the present moment.

MONDAY
Interference Patterns

*"We are infinitely removed from comprehending
the extremes, since the end of things; and their
beginning are hopelessly hidden from us in an
encapsulated secret. We are equally incapable of
seeing the Nothing from which we were made,
and the Infinite in which we are swallowed up."*
— *Blaise Pascal*

Nothing could soothe Khepri Livingston's disquieted soul more than a trip to the thrift store. Whenever she had a lot on her mind, it was the perfect place to go for a quick distraction. Getting lost down the aisles of clothes and shoes, Khepri felt she could hide her own mental clutter inside the bins and racks of old stuff.

When she touched the objects: picture frames, colorful glass bottles, trunks, suitcases, candelabras, dresses, pants, shoes, books, records, VHS tapes, she lost touch with her own problems. Her fingertips would vibrate with energy as she pondered where this thing or that thing had come from, what had been its journey into her hands. Each object had its own secret history, a story stored up inside of it, radiating from the center of its mass.

Today was one of those days when Khepri needed a strong dose of that thrift therapy. It was the first day of spring and her twenty-eight birthday. But it wasn't starting off very happy or refreshing. Her daily sun sign horoscope had predicted as much when she glanced at it on her phone, while brushing her teeth to get ready for work:

Be wary of misleading information and prepare for the potential need to redo projects you thought were complete. You could be dealing with delays and a general feeling of being held back.

And the horoscope was proving true, so far, from the moment she opened her eyes that Monday morning. She woke up to the irritating buzzer of an alarm she was supposed to have heard ten crucial minutes earlier, following a bad sleeping episode the night before.

The next glitch was the accident on the highway—probably the result of reckless driving in the sheets of rain blanketing the highway in the storm. She scolded herself for neglecting to look up the weather along with her astrological forecast.

Next came a less than subtle reprimand for lateness, arriving in her email inbox shortly after she arrived at her job as an investigative journalist at the independent media outlet *The Sun Times Journal*. It was sent by Sianne Sharpe, the managing editor in her department who wore a chip on her shoulder to work every day.

Once Khepri's 11 AM "anonymous source" failed to show up at her office, she was no longer under the illusion that the day would suddenly improve. Although she rarely used the little sick and vacation time she had, she decided to play sick the rest of day and escape to the other side of town. The destination was a thrift store she had never visited: *The Recycle Bin.*

The Recycle Bin hadn't been around long. A few weeks after moving into her two-bedroom apartment in historic Germantown late last year, a small, glossy, festive flier advertising an "Opening Sale-abration!" in purple, yellow, and black lettering was slipped into her mail-slot.

Khepri remembered reading it and wondering how the flier had even reached her, given the location. The store was in a small suburb near Bryn Mawr that she never really had a reason to travel to, with the forty minute drive and her demanding work schedule. She typically just settled for her usual thrift store haunts in the city, near her job in Center City or her apartment in Germantown.

Until now. Khepri turned her car into the parking lot of a small shopping center in a remote clearing off the highway. The center housed only the thrift store, a produce market, and a video game shop. The thrift store stood as the largest building sandwiched between the other two, boasting a flashing, fluorescent green sign that had the universal recycling sign: circling white arrows between the words *Recycle* and *Bin.*

There were only a few cars in the spaces in the shopping center lot. It was either a good time of the day to shop or this place was always dead. The drab-looking buildings told her it was probably the latter.

She pulled her hoodie over her head and walked inside to find a large, brightly-lit warehouse outfitted with gleaming metal racks and rows of shelves. A chill grazed her spine as her body adjusted to the drafty temperature in the building. The space was much larger than the crowded boutiques and overflowing store bins in the mom and pop thrifts she frequented.

The store was also unusually organized and neat— almost sterile. Items sat on the shelves, like artifacts labeled and filed away in a storage room. Spotlight-bright lights shone down into the aisles and bounced off the chalk white walls on to the black and white checker floor, which was nearly squeaky-clean enough to slide across.

It even smells *clean in here.*

Khepri detected an odor of pine-sol wafting up from the ground, instead of the usual smell of moth balls and dust scent she got in other stores. She could tell that this wasn't going to be the most charming thrift store she had ever patronized.

Only five or six shoppers were scattered around the large store, grannies leaning up against carts and moms rolling strollers across the wide aisles. Two cashiers sat at two adjacent registers near the front entrance: a boy and girl in their late teens or early twenties. The girl was twirling her honey-dipped loc'd hair around a fingertip, while popping gum and texting furiously on her phone — virtually ignoring her tall, skinny blonde co-worker babbling on about some video game he would get from next door with his next paycheck. Neither of them acknowledged Khepri's entrance, which she didn't altogether mind, given her irritable mood.

As was her ritual when shopping at a thrift store, Khepri looked around for the donation counter, finding it all the way at the back of the warehouse. According to a large green map hanging from chains in the ceiling at the front entrance, she was *now* **Here:** the white dot standing at the front. The map pointed the way to the Donation Center, located in the rear of the warehouse.

Whenever she went thrifting, Khepri always donated a bag of her own clothing, books, or furniture. Before she could assume the responsibility of adopting a recycled item into her home to instill it with new meaning and memories, she felt that she needed to sacrifice something of her own. She usually had a bag waiting in the trunk.

Out with the old and in with the new-to-me.

She walked back to the Donation Center, which was a large, wooden counter painted black with small piles of clothes and books spread out around the counter. The counter stood in front of what looked to be another large room. The entrance to this room was covered by a heavy, velvet curtain that she could not see behind, around, or under.

There was no one behind the counter and no employees near or around the Donation Center. With the size of the store and the music blaring out over the speakers, she thought it would be futile to call out. She also did not want to engage in any small talk with the clerks.

Khepri decided to plop her small bag of old clothes next to the other piles. It blended in perfectly.

Time to get lost.

She pushed her headphones into her ear, turned the player up, pulled her hoodie up even further over her 'fro she had earlier brushed back into a puffy ponytail, and pulled her shades down to hide her eyes.

She hoped to block out any part of the world that didn't include her favorite band screaming in her ears, vintage clothes, pre-owned books, and antique lamps.

After an hour of browsing the color-coded racks of clothing and systematically-arranged housewares to the tunes of *Black Privilege*, she found very few items of interest or to her taste. However, that hour of mindless browsing was just what she needed to work out ways to minimize the stress that had been predicted for her day. She was also enjoying spending a quiet birthday of quality time with herself. The thought of cooking had even crossed her mind, or, at the very least, ordering something different off the menu of one of her usual take-out spots.

She next made her way over to the bookshelves that spanned the length of one entire wall of the store. The book section was always the section she saved for last.

A thrift store book section had a special kind of magic for her for a very specific reason. On every visit, no matter which thrift store she went to, no matter how small or disheveled their book section, she would always, *always* find a favorite childhood book that she had lost over the course of growing up and moving around.

The books were mostly young adult novels or children's reference books. But each book was one that inspired her, propelled her in some way, or had otherwise been one of few sources of comfort, escape, and sanctity through a rough childhood.

In fact, the books seemed to be the only thing that reminded her that she had had a childhood at all. Much of her other memories of it had been lost or hidden in places she was not yet ready to examine.

Finding them again like that, in thrift stores, made her want to believe that the books were somehow being set out on purpose— by someone—just for her. The idea was farfetched, but she just couldn't explain how she never failed to be drawn right to the area where a childhood book sat; and how it would be there, waiting patiently. Or so it seemed.

Some days she even fancied that it was actually one of her previously-owned books that had made its way back into her hands, that the book had the same tattered corners and yellowing marks that her old books would have.

Although highly unlikely, it was plausible, since she had never written her name in her books as a kid, as her friends would do, had never made any marks out of what seemed a profound sense of respect for them. Of course, once she had gone to college, defiling books with ink had become a matter of necessity.

Foreign to Khepri's usual thrifting experiences, *The Recycle Bin* had its books sectioned off and neatly arranged into a few rigid categories: *History, Science, Philosophy,* and *Biography.* It seemed like a pretty limited, almost arbitrary, selection of categories, especially with no children's or fiction sections.

A little disappointed that she might not come across one of her favorites, Khepri fingered the spines of the books with her back to the rest of the store, musing on the titles. As she looked over them, she noticed that many of the books were actually familiar to her.

Several of the books were ones that she had used in researching articles at her job, had read in college, or that she was interested in reading someday.

Some of them could have been plucked right off the tall, mahogany bookcase that stood in her living room! Titles such as *History and Memory in African-American Culture, Astro-Mythology: The Celestial Union of Astrology and Myth* by Valerie Vaughan, and *Grammatical Man: Information, Entropy, Language and Life* by Jeffrey Campbell peppered the shelves of the book section.

Khepri turned around to cast suspicious glances at the few other shoppers in the store. It was the same five or six people, grandmoms and soccer moms, humming along to some Billy Joel song or whatever it was playing on the loudspeakers.

Judging by that crowd alone, and the little that she knew about the small suburban area surrounding the store, the shoppers did not seem like the types who would own books on African literature, Astrology, or Quantum Physics, but maybe a college student from the next town over had dumped off a bunch of books here one day.

She grabbed a few of the titles from each section and placed them in her cart until she rolled up to the last section, which was *Biography*. She didn't expect to find anything of interest.

Most thrift stores only had biographies of former first ladies or first-hand accounts of mountain-climbing expeditions. On the other hand, the other categories had already served up a few unexpected titles. Perhaps this one would as well.

As soon as she walked to the section, her eyes fell upon a small, thin, stapled-together book, sticking out squarely between other hardbacks. Curious, Khepri pulled it out from between, her brain registering a fleeting little tingle in her fingertips as she made contact with the book.

The book was crudely assembled, as if it had been printed out on someone's home computer, folded over horizontally into a book, and stapled together.

The cover read:

EXPERIMENTAL

TIME

ORDER

in bold, black letters, with no author listed. Small spiral symbols were centered above and beneath the title. There was nothing on the back cover.

Even more intrigued, Khepri flipped through the first few pages, finding a plain title page, then a table of contents. Further inside were snippets of poems, handwritten journal entries, densely typed paragraphs of text, appendices, and crude drawings of graphs, spirals, cubes, and other shapes.

There seemed to be no signs of the author's name on any of the opening pages, but there were various quotes by a few recognizable names throughout the book and some other names she had never heard of before.

She turned to the first page of the book and read:

Dear Reader,

I hope that you have picked up this book as I intended. If so, you are reading this message at the exact time that I mapped out for this, in your "now" moment. Using a precise arrangement of Bayesian statistics, quantum mechanics, astrology, and mental time travel, I have very carefully calculated every probability of how you should receive this book, and how you will respond to it.

If all of the right paths have been taken to lead you here and this book has timely made it into your hands, there is still a slim probability that you are in a timeline/universe where you dismiss this as a complete work of fiction, the work of a madman, or the work of a prankster. However, because you have read this far, you have already decided to continue reading. You made the decision to keep reading these words a few seconds before you were conscious of making the decision.

Before we continue, you must become meta-aware that you are a part of this book, and it is necessary that you retain your meta-awareness as you continue reading. You, the observer, must recognize that you must be included into the system that you are observing.

That's right. You are not only just reading words flat on a page, but you are in fact entangled with these words by the act of reading them, by the act of using the light of your eyes to see them, by the act of using your personal memory and context to give these words definition. By reading these words, you are constructing a bridge of time and space connecting you to me, allowing us to interact within the same frame of reference.[1]

As you will soon find out, this interaction is governed by physical law and, like any other law, physical laws can be reinterpreted, rebooted, and manipulated.

No more time can be spent on introductions, so I must trust that you will piece things together as you read further. Life as we know it may very well depend on you doing so.

You will see that I have compiled all of my notes, instructions, and diagrams in as organized an effort as time will allow. So the only thing left for you to do now is to turn the page.

---

[1] "Vision alone makes us learn that beings that are different, exterior, foreign to one another are absolutely together, are simultaneity." Maurice Merleau-Ponty

"What in the *world?*" Khepri wondered out loud, absurd questions bubbling up in her brain. This *had* to be a joke. But it was so somber. She didn't know whether to laugh, keep reading, or get as far away from it as possible.

The book felt eerily compelling, even in its obvious absurdity. Just like one of her childhood books that she would always find, this one seemed like it had been placed there strategically for her to come across— sticking out just *so*, just at the right time, like the introduction had said. Oddly enough, she didn't want to take the risk of ignoring it.

Khepri tried to shake the thoughts from her head, feeling a little silly about being spooked by the book. It was probably just some whacked out adult choose-your-own adventure-story zine someone had attempted. But she still couldn't ignore the way in which the writer had seemed to pinpoint where, when, and how she would come across the book.

In the end, interest won out over her reservations, and Khepri made up her mind to purchase it. In fact, she was anxious to get home and examine it closer.

Since nothing else in the thrift store promised to be as fun as her little time travel manual find, Khepri pushed her cart up to the front of the store, where the cashiers stood doing much of the same things they had been doing when she came in. She decided to try her luck on the furiously texting girl, whose name tag read: "Tonya."

As she approached the counter and begin putting items in front of Tonya's register, the teen put her phone down. Instead of grabbing an item to ring up, Tonya looked up at Khepri with sparkling tree bark-colored eyes, and flawless, sepia-toned skin.

Those eyes lingered on Khepri's a few moments too long, before Khepri broke the exchange, turning around to her cart to fumble for more items.

The stare, even though brief, had unnerved her a bit. But it hadn't just been the eye contact, she realized as she grabbed Experimental Time Order out of the cart. There had also been a weird, little, pursed-lip smirk that crept across Tonya's face as well, as if she were holding a secret.

Or, Khepri thought as she turned back around to face Tonya and put the book on the counter, *maybe I'm just imagining things*. The girl was back to paying her no mind, ringing up her purchases with one hand and checking on an audible, incoming text with the other.

***

Back at her apartment, Khepri sat down at the desk in her spare room, and turned on her laptop. As she waited for it to load, she looked around and shook her head at the swirl of clothes, shoes, boxes, and papers littering every available surface. The spare room promised to be an actual home office someday. For now, it multi-functioned as Khepri's dressing room, storage room, office, and guestroom if needed.

For as long as she'd known, she'd been contending with a defective memory which, combined with her own brand of neurosis, caused her to develop a habit of writing reminder notes to herself for some future event.

Every free inch of her refrigerator door, work and home desks were filled with little yellow sticky notes and sheets of notebook paper that read things like: *Dear Khep, don't forget to pick up dry cleaning on Fri.! Khep PLEASE pay the phone bill tomorrow,* or *Have story on Jack's desk by 6!*

Khepri preferred the illusion of bright, individual sticky notes that she could move around, throw away, stick and un-stick, to a perpetually long, enumerated to-do list.

Although she wanted to do nothing more at the moment than dig into the strange handbook that seemed to be speaking directly to her, she knew it would be prudent for her to handle a bit of business before leisure, so as not to pay hell the next day for playing hookey at work today.

She promised herself that she would answer just a few emails, reschedule some appointments and then take the rest of her birthday to do the things that her schedule tended to deny her most: relaxation and leisure reading.

Khepri was working on a big story about medical experimentation on teen boys in *Haverford Juvenile Detention Facility* located in Haverford County, just outside of Philly. A few leads had uncovered that the detention center was receiving large kickbacks from an institution conducting government research on violent behaviors, in exchange for "bodies"— teen boys they could run the experiments on.

The kickbacks, in turn, appeared to have ties to unusually high adjudication rates in the Philadelphia juvenile courts over the past few years.

Pieced together from several sources from within the facility, Khepri had learned that the researchers were investigating the statistical possibility that violent behavior was inherited in families, and trying to identify a possible biological or neurological basis for violence.

The study had targeted Black and Latino boys of color almost exclusively, and had gone on for at least four years. Khepri's team did not yet have the name of the institution. Her source, who was a no-show interview, was supposed to be bringing her a smoking gun piece of evidence that would identify the institution. She wasn't all that surprised that her informant didn't show up to the interview. His job, and possibly more, was on the line.

Experimentation of this sort was unfortunately neither uncommon nor unheard of. Khepri had read up on similar experiments that targeted young, Black children in *Medical Apartheid: The Dark History of Medical Experimentation on Black Americans from Colonial Times to the Present.* The book, written by Dr. Harriet Washington, outlined the excruciating details of medical experimentation performed on children as young as six by such esteemed institutions as University of Mississippi, Columbia University, and Baltimore, Maryland's Kennedy Krieger Institute.

The offenses ranged from injections with experimental vaccines and drugs, testing newborns for HIV without their mother's consent and withholding positive results, to lobotomies and removal of areas of the brain on young black boys.

What made the *Haverford Experiments* (as she had dubbed them) unusual from other stories she read about was that the researchers weren't using medication or surgery on the boys. The researchers in this case were apparently using some sort of non-invasive, brainwave-altering virtual video game device, which sounded like something lifted from the pages of a bad science fiction novel.

The story had fallen on Khepri's lap through an unusual channel. A product of the foster care system herself, Khepri often gave speeches and workshops at foster and youth transition homes, telling her story of aging out of foster care, going to college, and becoming a journalist. After one such speech six weeks ago, on Career Day at a teen transition home located in North Philly, one of the counselors, Jim Hernandez, pulled her aside to talk about some of the strange behaviors he noticed in some of the kids in the home.

Three of the boys had spent time between the home and the *Haverford Juvenile Detention Facility*. They had been put in the detention center for generally petty crimes—such as stealing clothes and possession of marijuana. Increasingly, however, the counselor noted changes in all three boys' behavior.

"The boys were troubled, no doubt," Hernandez told her, speaking in a hushed voice, his eyes darting around him. "Who wouldn't be, given their background and their family history— you know? But they were good kids, they still had a chance. No history of violence, nothing like that."

"But then strange things started happening to those boys, Miss. They kept coming back in here every six or seven months, but this time with violent crimes. One kid held up a lady at gunpoint, beat her in the head with the gun. Funny thing is, he didn't take any money from her, no jewelry, nothing. He just beat the shit out of her and ran off to the corner store. Bought him an orange soda and gulped it down like he just crawled from out of a desert—bloody hands and all.

I talked to these kids in depth when I went to visit them up at *Haverford*, Ms. Livingston. One boy said he felt brain sick. Like he was inside that game—like a Sims character being pulled down the street by a force beyond his control. Said it had something to do with some games the guards were making them play at *Haverford*," he said.

Khepri entertained the conversation, musing on the counselor's paranoia a few moments. It was definitely a strange story, but not implausible. The whole justice system was one big, strange conspiracy, as far as she concerned.

On the other hand, there was likely some other logical explanation for Hernandez's anecdotes about the boys. Besides, people always proposed story ideas and things that they thought she should investigate, once they found out what she did. Very few ideas panned out.

She told the counselor she would try to look into it, but it quickly slipped to the back cloud of her mind to join the other hundreds of story ideas floating around. Until about a week later.

She was combing *The Inquirer* for research on another story about voter ID laws, when she came across an article detailing a recent string of homicides and violent assaults concentrated in the twenty-second Police District of North Philly; with no clear ties to drugs or money. Further probing into names and other details of the crimes through some back channels, eventually led her back to the teen boys who had crossed through the *Haverford Juvenile Detention Facility*.

Pitching the story idea to the powers-that-be had been no picnic. Especially with only circumstantial evidence of a connection.

But after two review panels, it had been dubbed compelling enough to be given the "green-light." She was paired with a leading team member to help her with the investigation, her good friend and office mate Mark Bloom, under the supervision of Sianne Sharpe.

It was her first major assignment since starting at the *Sun Times* last fall, so the final article had to be a flawless piece of journalism, or her career would be damned. This particular article had heavy racial, legal, and political implications that were too hot for most of the other ass-kissing journalists to touch.

But Khepri wasn't afraid to get burned. It was the perfect opportunity for her to show she did not need an Affirmative Action pass. Being one of the youngest investigative journalists, one of the few females, and one of the very few people of color at the *Sun Times,* she stood at the intersection of two of the most disfavored categories of social existence, black and female, and she was not allowed to forget that at her job.

The *Sun Times* tried its best to appear as a "progressive" paper in the digital era, an appearance necessary to keep up with the lighting-quick pace of the internet news market. Its recent push to expand its platform included slightly edgier features, such as her story, and hiring practices that were more "diverse," in the most narrowly defined way possible.

But the truth was that the *Sun Times* was established in a bygone era. It was still owned and run by aging, moderately conservative white men stubbornly holding onto their privilege, writing for an audience that was still largely other aging, moderately conservative white men. Most of the other journalists with her title did not require two review panels for their stories to get an approval stamp - controversial or not.

Sianne Sharpe, a fire engine red-headed white woman, was also part of the female minority at the *Sun Times,* and the only female lead editor. She usually gave Khepri assignments that didn't really allow her to convey her skills as a researcher and writer, such as lottery ticket scams run by the local mom and pop shop, or pieces on new voter id laws. Stories interns could research and write.

Not allowing Khepri to shine only justified whatever preconceived notions her bosses had about her abilities, which threatened to become a dangerous, career-ending feedback loop.

Khepri was well aware that she had likely been hired to fill some quota, regardless of how well she could write, how well her leads panned out, or how thorough her research was. Her very presence was regarded as alien within the culture of the paper.

But whatever their reasons for bringing her on, she intended to make the best of her experiences there, and then move on to riper fruit. The inevitable controversy of her article on the *Haverford Experiments* promised to be her breakout piece. For better or worse.

It was only three PM, a few hours since Khepri had left the job that morning. But her work email had at least forty unopened messages.

"Big surprise," Khepri muttered dryly.

Under Sharpe's regime, she was in constant communication with the investigation team members. Sharpe had insisted upon her entire department getting cell phones equipped to receive work emails; preferably an iphone.

46

But Khepri felt that she was at the office and in front of a computer often enough to not need to carry her in-box around in her pocket. Besides, she was generally a low-tech, old school sort of girl. She had not yet upgraded her VCR to a DVD player, and had never bothered to open up the GPS device that she received as a Christmas gift one year.

Khepri poised herself to answer her emails, but then began to reason her way out of it. If she answered just a few emails, she would be compelled to answer all forty, *and* to follow up on whatever tasks were required therein.

No. I deserve some true me time, at least one day out of the year.

Khepri sent an email to her team members letting them know she wouldn't be in, before turning off her cell phone and left it on the desk. Khepri took the short walk down the hallway to relocate to the living room. On the way there she stopped in the kitchen to pour a glass of wine before fishing Experimental Time Order (or ETO, as she had started calling it in her head) from out of the plastic bag that held her purchases from *The Recycle Bin*. She curled up in her favorite spot in the corner of the sofa and opened it.

Touching the book again gave her the same tingly feeling she'd had when she first picked it up in the store. Not knowing whether the sensation was real or imagined, she brushed it off and casually flipped through the book again. The contents didn't seem so unusual to her, she supposed, after giving it another look. A few of the topics, such as time and memory, were topics she had researched during her days a research assistant in college.

What appeared strange about the little book, if anything, was the way it was all pieced together. Theories, formulae, quotes, article clippings, journal-style ramblings all thrown in — with no author claiming the work. Not to mention the introductory letter that read like the handiwork of a deteriorating schizophrenic.

It all seemed like a monumental waste of time to even attempt to decipher it. However, she was admittedly hooked in by its quirkiness, and wondering how the anonymous author interpreted the topics sprinkled throughout the book.

Or is it something more?

On some level, the book felt like it was speaking directly to her, looking into her like a mirror. She took a sip of wine and turned to Chapter One: Experimental Time Order.

Chapter One:

Experimental Time Order

The Brain

The brain "holds" non-material information and stores it up in a holographic computer. There is lots of evidence that our brain stores information like a hologram. "This storage device is the most compact known in Nature. An example of this is the genetic code carried in our chromosomes. Each cell in our bodies carries all the information required to make an additional copy of our bodies," says Itzhak Bentov.

The brain functions as a recording device for images/electromagnetic pulses. If we are shown a picture or image, we continue to see that image for $1/10^{th}$ of a second after it has been taken away–this means that the brain is working with old visual information. Some scientists believe that the brain may have evolved to see a split second into the future when it perceives motion, given the $1/10^{th}$ of a second delay in modeling visual information.

Films and movies take this concept to create moving pictures. In films, a moving object is broken down into a series of still pictures. This is the illusion of motion.

"It takes time for the brain to process visual information, so it has to anticipate the future to perceive the present" —Mark Changizi

If the brain is shown two images in quick succession, such as a picture of a dot on the left side of the image, and then a picture of a dot on the right side of the image, the brain will see motion from left to right, even though there was no motion. When shown two images in quick succession, one of a dot on the left of a screen and one with the dot on the right, the brain sees motion from left to right, even though there was none.

In one experiment, designed by Dr. Romi Nijhawan, people watch an object pass a flashbulb. The timing is exact: the bulb flashes as soon as the object passes. However, people in the experiment consistently perceive that the object has moved past the bulb before it flashes. [2]

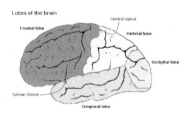

---

[2] See Anticipating the Future to 'See' the Present by Benedict Carey, 6/10/08
http://www.nytimes.com/2008/06/10/health/research/10mind.html?_r=0

"The brain. . . is that which allows the mind to adjust itself exactly to circumstances. It is the organ of attention to life. Should it become deranged, however slightly, the mind is no longer fitted to the circumstances; it wanders, dreams. Many forms of mental alienation are nothing else. But from this it results that one of the roles of the brain is to limit the vision of the mind, to render its action more efficacious. This is what we observe in regard to the memory, where the role of the brain is to mask the useless part of our past in order to allow only the useful remembrances to appear. Certain useless recollections, or dream remembrances, manage nevertheless to appear also, and to form a vague fringe around the distinct recollections. It would not be at all surprising if perceptions of the organs of our senses, useful perceptions, were the result of a selection or of a canalization worked by the organs of our senses in the interest of our action; but that there should yet be around those perceptions a fringe of vague perceptions, capable of becoming more distinct in extraordinary, abnormal cases. Those would be precisely the cases with which psychical research would deal." - Dreams by Henry Bergson

The Eye and Vision

Some theories of vision state that vision begins when light strikes the photoreceptive cells in the retina. The optic nerve bends light and interprets the electromagnetic pulse. Four types of photoreceptive cells in the retina react to different wavelengths and intensities of light. Each eye takes in a different slice of the visual world, which is processed in the opposite brain hemisphere. It is then integrated into a coherent image.

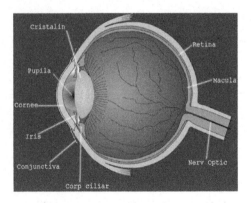

We can only see things by way of light, which is why nothing can exceed the speed of the rate which we can perceive it. We only see into the future as far as light can travel. We see into the past at the speed of thought.

Slowed light + present light allows you to receive images from the past in the present

To perceive the world is to anticipate it. In many ways, the eye acts like a camera. The clear picture from a camera is produced by moving the lens nearer or further away from the film. The eye has a similar lens, the crystalline lens. The eye uses this to focus pictures. Also like a camera, the eye controls the amount of light passing through the lens.[3] If you look into a mirror at one of your own eyes you will see the light control the iris. In other ways, the eye (in conjunction with the brain) is creative and active in perceiving the world[4] Vision is a quantum experience, like a wave-particle duality. We can see things within our field of vision as one whole scene, and we can discern things within our field of vision as separate parts.

---

[3] "Astronomy provides the hypothesis of capturing images of the past by means of the time gap between the emission and reception of the light emitted by far-off stars." – Camille Flammarion, Astronomer. In his novel Lumen, "retrospective vision incorporated the movement of the observer, who goes back in time faster than the speed of light, whereas synchronizing the speed with the speed of light allows him to isolate a picture (Cinema Beyond Film: Media Epistemology in the Modern Era)."

[4] A passive, mirror-like eye would simply receive the world and add nothing of its own, but the human eye...is creative as well as receptive..[meaning] that the colorful world takes some of its coloration from the eye and that interior productions of the eye—so-called optical illusions-are as real and as worthy of study as sights streaming in from the outside."

For example, we sit in a room, and from where we sit in the room, we can see the couch we sit on, the television in front of us, the book in our hand, the words we read. That is an entire scene. Within that scene, however, we see each thing as a separate part, for the individual object that it is. When we see objects or items within our field of vision, all of those things coexist within one frame of vision simultaneously and non-causally.

As I write this, the book I am writing in, the pen I am writing with, and the room I sit in all exist within my frame of vision; with no delay and no causality. Light brings all of these items into my vision at one time. There is no cause and effect involved in having both the pen and book and room in my field of vision. Light shows me all of these things at one time, as an even whole presented as my visual field. [5]

---

[5]"Visual context is a precondition for seeing, and such context presupposes the gathering together of objects that may strike us as unrelated, even randomly aggregated. But this gathering-together signifies a deeper articulation to the world than causality with its assumption of self-standing parts or particles. That assumption takes us just so far, but then the parts organize in non-causal ways, and without that organization the world would be much less intelligible. . .As Maurice Merleau-Ponty puts it: 'Vision alone makes us learn that beings that are different, exterior, foreign to one another are absolutely together, are simultaneity [in your visual field]'" Grandy, David. Everyday Quantum Reality. Bloomington: Indiana UP, 2010. Print.

Light also shows me these things instantly. There is no delay in vision —most people immediately apprehend what their eyes look at. There is no space, no time, between your eyes looking at a thing in your visual field and actually seeing that thing. "n the moment of experience, we do not wait for images to travel across space and time," says David Grandy.

Time = when we notice change. We notice change when light reaches the eye and the brain processes that visual information.

Light, Pt. 1

How does light "reach" the eye? Does it need to travel? If it travels faster than anything we can know of, is it really traveling? If light is outside space-time, not belonging to it because it exceeds it, how can light be said to move at all? Or is light always there, blanketing the background, or perhaps, the fabric that holds the background together?

Light has a limiting speed, but that speed is universal. Because nothing can exceed the speed of light, light itself exists outside of any notion of speed, becoming the backdrop against which any speed in the knowable universe, is measured, thus defining its own speed. [6]

c = speed of light | Speed of light = c

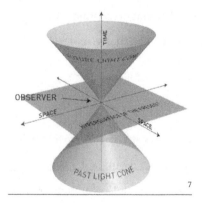

It is a circular definition—self confirming, and self referencing.

Light must stand outside of reality in order to reflect it.

---

[6] We don't see light traversing space and time; we infer its space-time movement upon performing the experiment...It does not show up on its own in [the space-time] universe, furthermore it is not part of that universe when moving at its own speed, according to Einstein. At that speed, writes John Wheeler keying off of Einstein, light makes 'zero-interval linkages between events near and far,' an expression that calls to mind nonlocality or quantum entanglement." (Grandy, 2)

[7]"Light...intrinsically covers one meter of distance in one meter of time; it is the trajectory at which space and time perfectly offset each other and thereby cancel out. Accordingly, "the interval between two events is zero when they can be connected by one light ray." (Grandy, 2010)

The human eye can detect changes in the intensity
of **light**, not, however, the wavelength because light
oscillates too fast (approximately 1000 trillion times
per second). [8]

The eye is perfectly constructed to interpret light, creating the phenomenon of vision

Nothing else can travel faster than light, nothing else can achieve c,
light speed, except *light*. We would need light in order to "see"
whatever signal would outrace the light. And because we cannot
observe faster than light, we cannot see light surpass itself to
arrive it. Thus we limit light to speed c, which it cannot surpass
(go faster than) c, because it *is* c.

Has anyone ever seen light move, pure light, the light that allows
you to see other light sources, for instance, a light bulb or sun?
The light that allows you to see darkness? How can we see before
seeing?

This is why the observer must always be a part of the experiment.
Nothing will outpace light. Because the observer is bound by light
to the experiment, he can never be truly objective. Light levels the
playing field for everyone, since the observer will always need light
to see. Light is the observer of all. Yet, contradictorily, the act of
seeing, vision, immediately cuts across space-time to give our eyes
immediate contact with the object we are looking at.

---

[8] Light Oscillations Become Visible" http://phys.org/news977.html#nRlv

Mirrors

A mirror is one of the easiest ways to reflect light and alter the speed of light to slow it down. Mirrors will allow you to see images several seconds back into the past.

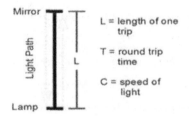

"*I say that for some, mirrors constitute a hieroglyph of truth in that they uncover everything which is presented to them, like the habit of truth which cannot remain hidden. Others, on the contrary, hold mirrors for a symbol of falsity because they so often show things other than as they are.*" – Raphael Mirami

I cannot "see" myself without a reflection. But yet, the reflection is an image which is not looking at anything and the self is not observing the self as seen in reverse. The image on the other side of the mirror does not return the gaze.

Science has yet to unlock the vast powers of the mind by failing to do one simple thing—acknowledge the experimenter, the observer, the scientist, the living man as involved with the experiment, the thing being observed.

The observer effect and mirrors— the seer can see itself/the witness can watch itself/the observe can observe itself/the awareness can be aware of itself. Observations always precede their theories, never in reverse.

Theories are tailored to their experiments
Interdependent, well-rehearsed
Subjectivity cannot be minimized

Before you continue, please complete the following experiments.

Experiments:

1. *Stand two mirrors upright to form a right angle. When two mirrors are at right angles, the reflections bounce from one mirror to the other, creating multiple images. When the mirrors are facing each other, the reflections continue to bounce from one mirror to the other. You will be able to see reflections stretching back into infinity. Although your eyes cannot account for infinity reflections, you sense the depth and length.*

2. *Take a small clock, such as an alarm clock or kitchen clock or watch and place it in front of the mirror before you. Set the clock ten minutes fast.*

3. *Seat yourself or stand in front of the mirrors in a darkened room with a small flickering light, such as a candle or flashlight. Create a vacuum in the room by sealing it from excess light and sound coming from outside the room. Relax your body completely and breathe rhythmically and deeply.*

4. *Begin looking at your image in the mirror, concentrating*

   your attention intently upon your
   eyes without blinking.

5. *Repeat the words Who am I, where*
   have I been? into the mirror over
   and over until you no longer
   recognize the words

6. *If you take each reflections to your left as the past and*
   reflections to your right as the future, and use each
   reflection to signify one day, you can see yourself
   yesterday and yourself tomorrow, or as far ahead or
   behind as you wish. Your images in the mirror should
   morph, the further back or forward you look.

7. *To conclude the exercise, count backwards from ten.*
   When you get to 1, you will be fully back in the present.

YOU HAVE MADE CONTACT. STOP HERE UNTIL YOU

RECEIVE THE NEXT INSTRUCTION.

60

TUESDAY

The Defining I

*"When I think of me, I am me; when I think of me and you, I am
me and you; when I think of you alone, I am not there anymore;
when I think of God, I am God. What I see with my eyes closed
and with my eyes open is the same stuff: brain circuitry."*
– Robert Anton Wilson

The next morning, Khepri walked briskly into her tiny
office twenty-three minutes late, clutching ETO in one hand,
and her daily cup of *Dunkin Donuts* tea and paper bag,
holding a blueberry muffin with extra butter, in the other.

She nearly dropped the tea on Mark Bloome, her
office-mate and supervisor on her article, as she squeezed
past his chair to reach her desk against the opposite wall.

"Girl, I know you had better watch it! This is *silk,*
baby," he said, swiveling in his chair and dramatically
smoothing out the sleeves of his salmon pink shirt.

"Good morning to you too, Mark. Sheesh!"

"Yeah, it'll hopefully be an even better morning now
that you're here. Your little impromptu mental health day
yesterday wreaked havoc upon all the rest of us."

"Shit, what happened? I only had had one interview
on the schedule and he was a no-show."

She quickly moved around the organized chaos of
paper piled up on her desk to uncover her large desk calendar.

"Um, apparently you didn't, honey bunches, because
Mr. Anonymous Jones came at one pm on the dot for his
interview *and* his payment, and you were nowhere on Planet

Earth to be found. You're lucky I was here! I call you, your phone's off. I email you, there's no response."

"Oh nooo, Mark! I thought that interview was at eleven! I waited for nearly half an hour before I took off. I called him, and no answer."

"Yeah well, it was at one, on his lunchbreak. Really it's your own fault, Khep. I damn nearly spent an hour with your narrow, brown caboose trying to teach you how to synch your calendar with your Outview email account to your phone, *and* the office laptop from your home desktop! What happened?"

"Mark, now you know I'm a little slow with the technology." Khepri said.

"You ain't never lied, ya damn technophobe. You were the last investigator to graduate to a digital recorder for your interviews," he said.

"Yes, and I miss my old analogue tape recorder. It was nice and simple - stop, play, rewind, and fast forward. That was all I needed. I don't need all the folders and the uploading and the whose-it what-nots. Speaking of which, where is my recorder?"

She rummaged around in her right hand drawer, where she usually locked it up at the end of the day, but it was nowhere to be found. She started growing a little anxious. She wouldn't be able to get much done without it, and her spare was at home.

Mark rolled his eyes. "Whatever girl. I know one thing, you had better get it together, sooner rather than later. I know yesterday was your birthday, but you've been slacking off the past week or so on your deadlines. You know Sharpe the Dart is going to notice sooner or later. And I am not going to keep covering for you, on *your* story. Humph! I am too pretty to be stressed-out. Or jobless," he told her.

Mark, who had been at the paper almost four years, worked his way up from local sports and business reporter to becoming one of the lead investigators. Being openly gay and Black, he always expressed empathy for the pressures and slights from their colleagues that Khepri had to deal with.

But, as she always reminded him, being a man provided him with a cushion, even if it was thinner than that of his white male counterparts. He seemed to have a lot more in common with the white men in the building as a man — *period* —than he did with her as a Black woman. Feeling that was bad enough, she dared not add her *own* sexuality into the mix. It would just be another topic to bristle about or throw "executive shade" at, like her natural hair and visible tattoos.

The story on the *Haverford Experiments* was Khepri's first real chance to prove she wasn't at the *Sun Times* on an affirmative action pass. It was also an opportunity for Mark, who had his eye trained on an editor position, to prove his chops with leading the team. Often working as Sharpe's proxy, he was the lead on Khepri's story, as well as the lead on another one of their colleague's stories.

She ignored his snide comment and let out a loud sigh, searching around the surface of the desk for the recorder.

"Yeah, if you were utilizing your downloadable mp3 files, you wouldn't be sweating right now. But here's something to brighten up your day. I thought you'd be happy to get this exclusive piece of info straight from the desk of the warden at the facility, as Mr. Jones had promised. Don't they know by now that information can neither be created nor destroyed?" he chuckled at his little joke, handing her a copy of a memo.

She snatched it out of his hands greedily. "Mark, this is great! We have a *name!* Actually, several," she said as she read over the memo. "Our legal department is going to have a field day with this one—this breaches all sorts of confidentiality of juvenile court records laws. But what's P.U.?"

"Our source revealed that it was some sort of school or college. I did some digging around and found one Parallel University in Bryn Mawr. One of those New Age deals, transformative, spiritual, manifest your own educational path colleges, blah blah blah. But apparently, its pretty well-respected. It has all of your standard majors and departments. They've won all kinds of awards, some government grants. I'll regale you with the necessary details later today after I make a few more contacts."

"Yes, I am quite familiar with Parallel U., actually," she said, swallowing thickly. "I, uh, took a few courses there when I was in high school."

"*You* would have. You never told me that."

"Yeah, I guess I didn't really remember until just now, as you said the name. It was over a summer, when I was a teen. Some college prep program or something."

Khepri's brain scrambled trying to search for more memories, information, images, anything about her time at the school. But she came up blank, save for a few fuzzy images of a younger version of herself sitting in a classroom or walking around the university. It was an eerie feeling, to be completely unfamiliar with experiences that she factually knew she had.

This must be what reverse déjà vu feels like.

"Well, I'll let you work the follow-up then, and I'll try to work Mr. Jones to get some more classified info," Mark said with a wink.

"On it." She opened her left hand desk drawer to retrieve a pen. In the drawer, inside of her pen bin was her tape recorder.

Hmm. Maybe Mark had been looking for something and moved it, even though he doesn't have a key to the drawer.

"So anyway, after all of that, how was your birthday day off? Didya get laid?," he asked her.

"Ha, no. My day was. . .interesting," she said.

"Oh? How's that?" he asked, engrossed in the interviews that he was coding.

She glanced over at Experimental Time Order, sitting on her desk.

Knowing his probable reaction, Khepri was hesitant to bring up the book. With a Masters in Statistical Analysis and plans to pursue his Ph.D, Mark's approach to their work, and to life in general, was methodical, matter of fact, and no-nonsense.

She always found it ironic that he was interested in working in what often proved, against everyone's best intentions, to be a highly subjective field. But he always claimed he was only interested in letting the numbers tell their own story and "setting the facts straight."

On the other hand, perhaps a rational second opinion was what she needed.

Mark cleared his throat, interrupting her thoughts. "Interesting how?" he repeated.

"So, I went to that new thrift store. It's actually kinda near Bryn Mawr. *The Recycle Bin.*"

"Doesn't ring a bell, honey. You know I'm allergic to thrift," Mark said.

"That's right, excuse me. Yeah, it's some new thrift store that I've been meaning to go to, but never had the time," she said.

"So the one day you decide to play hooky, that's how you choose to spend it? And on your birthday, no less. Khepri, I am disappointed in you, my sister. Was it worth your while?"

"Well," Khepri swallowed, "I found this strange little book on. . .time traveling."

"Hmm, come again?" Mark looked across the room at her then, squinting behind his designer reading glasses.

She walked over to his desk and dropped the book down in front of him. "It's a 'manual' on time travel. I found it at the thrift store. No author or anything. Take a look."

"Khepri, please toss this crap in the trash, get out of my face, and get to work," he said, thrusting the book back into her hands. He swiveled his desk chair around to face his computer again.

"Don't turn your back on me, jerk! You have to admit, it's kind of strange. Where could it have come from?," she asked.

"Girl, look, I admit nothing strange about it," he scoffed, turning back to look at her. "I'll tell you exactly what this little booklet is. Some crackpot conspiracy theorist put together a stupid little pamphlet of all their weirdo ideas, made a bunch of copies and put them in the one place somebody would pick it up. Sounds like just the kind of person who would be hanging around in a thrift store, anyway, and you sound like just the kind of person to buy it and eat it up. First, you're an astrologist. Now you wanna be time traveling," Mark said.

"Its not a weirdo idea when you have your nose buried in the Metro every morning reading you and your Derrick's horoscope, is it?" Khepri said. "Which, by the way, is only the horoscope for your sun sign, and is—"

"Guess what? I don't care, Khep! I only read it for fun. You're really into it," he interrupted.

He was right. For her, astrology carried the same utility as checking the weather. By being forewarned about the direction nature was destined to take, she felt forearmed to deal with the daily obstacles that might come her way. She usually read her horoscope religiously, like a daily scripture.

However, with work bearing down heavy the past few weeks, she hadn't had an opportunity to give more than a quick glance at her daily sun sign horoscope, which was about as comprehensive as cracking open a fortune cookie.

"Well, I don't care what you say either," she shot back on the way back to her desk. "This is weird shit, man. Look, it even talks about Bayesian probabilities—something you and I have talked about."

"Yeah, even more reason to reject it. You know I think Bayesian statistics is pure and utter feel good, layman's bull. I went to school for several years to study classical statistics and numbers, and there is nothing subjective about them. You know my motto. Say it with me now."

She chimed in sarcastically: "Numbers don't lie, people do. Yeah, yeah." Based on his reaction, Khepri decided not to mention that she had tried the first few exercises in *Chapter 1* of the book last night. . .

It had felt like she was getting ready to cast a magic spell.

After rummaging around in a utility drawer and her desk drawer, Khepri gathered the necessary materials: a small flashlight, a small digital kitchen clock, a red marker, and a desk calendar.

Khepri's apartment was a turn-of-the-century brownstone converted into apartments and duplexes, located in a historic part of the city. The apartment came with a stone fireplace, built-in book-shelves, a small private balcony, and other relics of the time, all for a monthly rent that an investigative journalist could afford.

One of the more unusual, antiquated features was a walk-in closet in her bedroom, with two doors standing side by side, opening up into opposite ends of the closet. Both doors had full-length mirrors embedded into them.

When she opened the two doors at the same time, the two mirrors stood before each other at right angles, like a pair of dressing room mirrors. She could position them just so that she could see the back of her body, and on into infinity, as the mirrors reflected off of one another. It made it easier to get dressed and do her hair in the mornings.

She did not allow herself to think too long about how the book assumed that she would have access to two mirrors of this type to perform the experiments.

Instead, she turned off all the lights in the bedroom and pulled close the heavy drapes to "seal the room from excess light," simulating a vacuum. She then pulled the closet doors open and positioned herself before the mirrors as the manual instructed, with the clock positioned so that the numbers appeared inverse. She had set it for ten minutes behind. She also set up the flashlight in front of the mirrors, after first moving it around in a spiral motion so as to open a light pathway in the mirrors, as ETO instructed.

She stared into the mirror, holding her own gaze hostage, into her millions of selves blurred into one, until the words "*I am*" blended into one motion rolling off her tongue and echoing into a supernova inside and around her head. She became paralyzed inside that gaze, the gaze in turn reflecting her own eyes. She could not move.

Thinking about the exercise now, she felt as though she were still there, locked in the mirror, as if no time had passed at all. . .

Khepri shook her head hard in an attempt to pull herself back to the present. She was in her office with ETO in her hands. The words on the cover danced around on the page for a moment, mocking her. She squinted and rubbed her eyes. They stood still again.

"You're probably right, Mark. I'm tired, stressed, and I'm more impressionable than usual. It's just a stupid little book. I'll leave it alone." Khepri slipped it inside of her desk drawer.

"You're damn right, I'm right. That's what friends are for— to be the voice of reason in the midst of madness and crazy talk. Now shred the damn thing and get started on your sections so that we can get out of here at a decent time tonight!"

"Why, what's so special about tonight? I planned on having a hot and steamy date with my laptop. We're going to do it in the library, on our favorite desk, mmm," she said, blowing loud kisses into the air.

"Girl, you really are losing it. We're supposed to be meeting Laura in Chinatown for your belated birthday drinks tonight! I'm sending a reminder alarm to your calendar right now, so just make sure you accept it. I got's to do everything around here, chile, I tell ya. "

A moment later, the reminder alarm dialogue box chimed on her computer. The noise and pop-up screen prompted a sudden flash of déjà vu, as if the ghost of a memory had passed by her and brushed up against her consciousness. The remembrance washed over her like an ocean wave, the assimilation of memory of a moment relived.

She felt the hairs along the back of her spine flex and quiver as her bones tingled. There were a few seconds of dizziness during which tiny points of blue, spectral light invaded her vision. A dense hollow sound drummed in her ears.

"Oh. . .oh, yeah. Yes, I know. Seven PM at *Hans,* that's right," she responded mechanically. He shot her a dubious look, but the response seemed to satisfy him. When he turned back around to return to his work, she brought up the Microbright Outview calendar on her computer to look turn off the reminder,

Once the calendar program loaded, a dialogue box containing appointment reminders popped up. First on the list were past due appointments from the previous days, and reminder alarms for all the appointments within the next twenty-four hours. Mark always lauded the calendar as the investigative journalist's best friend— particularly because it allowed you to enter dates and appointments onto the calendar retroactively, and created a timeline spreadsheet. Khepri, however, thought writing it out by hand was less tedious.

Khepri scrolled through the reminder box. She saw the reminder alarm for drinks at *Hans.* Right above that alarm, however, was a curious reminder alarm set to go off in the next 15 minutes, at ten AM. There was no name for the appointment. Khepri double-clicked on the alarm to see if there were any memos associated with it. She had to keep herself from falling off of her chair when it popped up and she read the memo in the appointment:

If you are reading this now, the experiments worked. Advance to Experimental Time Order, Chapter 2.

After first turning around to make sure that Mark wasn't looking, Khepri quietly pulled ETO back out of the drawer and found Chapter 2.

Experimental Time Order

Chapter 2

Although we know the sun does not revolve around the Earth, and that the universe does not revolve around the sun, science treats the universe as if it revolves around the Earth because all assumptions made about space are derived from human observation, human experience, and our imposition of our perceptions upon the macrocosms. If we could only admit to the limitations of our assumptions and perceptions, the "universe" as we call it, may be more willing to yield to our insatiable inquiries, our thirst for knowledge, our incessant measurements and observations.

Light, pt. 2

"Everything that happens. . .happens in the same 'one world' and is a part of it. For this reason events must possess an apriori aspect of unity."

– Carl Jung

No object can travel faster than the speed of light.[9] This simply means that no object can be observed traveling faster than SOL because we need light in order to observe the object and light always precedes/outruns its own observation.

We cannot separate light from our observation of it because we need it in order to see and observe. Light allows the eye to touch any object it falls upon without physically interacting with it. The act of seeing is to touch it. This allows seeing to be a quantum phenomenon.[10]

---

[9] "Dr. Edward Harris Walker suggests that what does move faster than light, and holds the Whole System together, is consciousness." – Wilson, Robert Anton, and Israel Regardie. Prometheus Rising. Phoenix, AZ: New Falcon Publications, 1997. Print., p. 246

[10] "Lights interactive vastness shows up wherever light shows up, and because no observer can back away from light or step outside its integrative embrace, different parts of light (photons) cannot be lifted out of the observation as distinct – i.e. distinctly observed- entities." – "Light as a Solution to Puzzles about Light." Journal for General Philosophy of Science / Zeitschrift Für Allgemeine Wissenschaftstheorie 33.2 (2002):369-79. JSTOR. <http://www.jstor.org/stable/10.2307/25171238?ref=search-gateway:791921333fa5ff95260df8cc5089d46d>

Photons - if a photon allows you to see other things, the photon itself cannot be seen. Otherwise you would not be able to see other things. 11

Key Quantum Physics Principles

Wave-Particle Dualism	The Wave-Particle Duality theory states that waves can exhibit particle-like properties while particles can exhibit wave-like properties. This definition opposes classical mechanics or Newtonian Physics
Quantum Superposition	Holds that a particle exists partly in all its particular, theoretically possible states (or, configuration of its properties) simultaneously; but, when measured or observed, it gives a result corresponding to only one of the possible configurations
Wave-function Collapse	The phenomenon in which a wave function—initially in a superposition of several states—appears to reduce to a single state after interaction with an observer. It connects the wave function with classcal observables like position and momentum. Collapse is one of two processes by which quantum systems evolve in time.

11 "A pair of quantum systems using photons in an entangled state can be used as a quantum information channel to perform computational, communication and cryptographic tasks that are impossible for classical systems. And, crucially for communications purposes, because the photon pairs are intrinsically linked, they provide complete security and fidelity - as when one photon is measured it reveals with absolute certainty what the other photon would reveal if measured. In addition, if the signal were intercepted by a third party it would immediately be detected, as the entanglement would have to be broken in order to intercept the message. Once the entanglement is broken, it cannot be restored." – Crystal Quantum Memories for Quantum Communication, **http://m.phys.org/news/2013-09-crystal-quantum-memories.html**

Non-locality of Quantum Particles	2 entangled particles behave as a single physical object, no matter how far apart they are. If a measurement is performed on one of these particles, the state of its distant twin is instantaneously modified.
Time symmetry	time is symmetrical for particles, meaning events happen the same way if time progresses forward or backward. For example, a video of two particles colliding and scattering off each other can be played forward or backward, and makes sense either way.

> The fact that quantum systems, such as electrons and protons, have indeterminate aspects means they exist as possibilities rather than actualities. This gives them the property of being things that might be or might happen, rather than things that are. This is in sharp contrast to Newtonian physics where things are or are not, there is no uncertainty except those imposed by poor data or limitations of the data gathering equipment.

In Prometheus Rising, R.A. Wilson talks about a popular thought experiment among California occultists involving a Magic Room with an Omniscient Computer. In the experiment, you are to project yourself in imagination inside this Magic Room and visualize the Omniscient Computer. The computer is built to respond instantly to human brainwaves, reading and decoding the meaning of the brainwaves. You only need to think in order to talk to the computer. You start off by asking the computer questions, starting from easy to increasingly more difficult. R.A.W. states that "almost everybody remembers the name of their first grade teacher" due to imprint vulnerability, "but that of the second grade teacher tends to get lost." Eventually, after experimenting with the easy questions, you can use the computer to explain the behavior of another person (i.e.

translate their reality-tunnel to you long enough for you to understand how events seem to them), perform analysis on obscure or paradoxical ideas for you, or even run meta-programs.

There are those who are capable of working backwards from reality. Taking something that they want to be true, and shaping the environment to fit that, creating a whole new fabric to overlay the first reality. What lies at the bottom, few can tell.

Experiments

1. *If you have not yet received the letter from experiment 2, use an electronic calendar or set an electronic alarm for one hour in the past. In the message, tell yourself to read Chapter 2 of Experimental Time Order.*

2. *If you have just received the message in experiment one, write a letter to your self, two days in the future. The letter should be put in a place you check regularly, such as a planner, diary or a journal. To convince yourself that it is you, tell yourself the name of your second grade teacher.*

3. *Change something small, but noticeable in your environment (i.e. moving an object out of its normal spot, setting a clock a few minutes off).*

These experiments will help you to position yourself in time relative to your past and future selves.
Do not read ahead until you receive a communication.

Khepri could barely get through the rest of the work day. Any other time she would have been really excited to receive such key information for her piece. She could now match names and arrest dates to the names of the boys listed in the memo.

They could finally start strategizing about who to interview, and what questions to ask. Given the surprising connection to Parallel U., and her *own* connection to the school, she should have been going through her list of contacts and her mental rolodex of things she already knew about the school.

Instead, her mind was fixated on thoughts of ETO, *Chapter 2's* exercises, and the bizarre message in her Outview calendar. Who had set up that appointment, prompting her to read *Chapter 2?* How had she received it before reading the chapter? Was she supposed to do *experiment 2,* since she had not sent herself the message in *experiment 1?*

It could have been a joke, but she didn't know who, or how that was possible. No one knew that she had picked the book up, besides Mark, and he made it abundantly clear that he wanted no parts of it.

There was also a peripheral piece of her that considered whether or not her sanity had come tumbling down, without grace and without warning.

Potential craziness aside, Khepri couldn't help considering the possibility, albeit highly remote, that this was all somehow real. She had at least been open-minded enough to, first of all, pick up the book, and second, try the experiments in *Chapter 1*. She had, without a doubt, received the message in Outview, and she had not, without a doubt, left the message there.

So if this was all real, and if she planned on writing a letter to herself two days in the future with any expectation of making contact with a "future self," whatever that could mean, she had to understand how it all worked.

She also knew that she would forever wonder what would happen if she didn't do it. The curiosity would be unbearable. Her curiosity was part of the reason she became a researcher and journalist— a curiosity that drove her, a constant search for something, the fear that she would miss something. Or that something was lost that only she could recover.

The time travel manual seemed to speak directly to this drive in her. Which made her wonder if she really had a choice in any of this at all. She kept pondering on how the manual and its anonymous author seemed to know that she would be compelled to try the experiments. Had the book and its author sought her out intentionally for this?

After suffering through drinks with Mark and Laura, Khepri faked enough yawns to be released. She needed to get home in time to think through *what* she would write in the letter. She already knew where she would write it: her dream journal.

Khepri's deep interest in astrology and other esoteric topics extended itself to the dream world. She was usually pretty disciplined about keeping the dream journal, a habit she had picked up along the way as a college student, after spending hundreds of work-study hours as a research assistant, interview transcriber, and many other research-related odd jobs.

Work on the *Haverford Experiments* the past few weeks had allowed this practice to fall into negligence as well, even though the story she was writing prompted some of her more dark and difficult sleeping patterns. Khepri was prone to nightmares and sleep paralysis, disorders that only increased during times of high stress.

Ironically, though, Khepri's last entry in her dream journal had been two days ago, on Sunday, March twentieth, a few minutes before midnight, after trying to wake up from a series of *dream within a dream* phantasms that had subsequently ended in sleep paralysis.

She turned now to the middle of the journal where a pen sat, serving as a bookmark in the space where she wrote that entry. She glanced briefly at her last entry before thumbing to a fresh page, shuddering a bit as she read it and recalled the sleep paralysis episode.

The entry ended on the right hand side of the page.

However, the next page was not blank, as it should have been.

Where there should have been a white page interspersed with thin black lines, there was instead a neatly written entry, beginning on the left side of the page, covering both sides of the pages in the journal, like a letter. This was quite unlike her typical entries, which were short, choppy, and scribbled in an effort to get down as many details about her dreams as quickly as possible.

But she immediately recognized the handwriting on the page as her unmistakable own, when she was trying to write legibly in a hurry. A split second after that recognition, the corner of her eye caught the corner of the page, where the date was scrawled. And her heart dropped to the bottom of her stomach.

The entry was dated for Thursday, March twenty-fourth. Two days from *now:* forty-eight hours from now, to be exact.

She sat on her bed, struggling to hold onto the journal in her trembling hands, squinting at the words on the page:

Thursday, March 24th, 10:45pm

Dear Khepri,

I don't know if you're going to receive this or not. Hopefully this will work out the way I envisioned it. If it does work, you're reading this after I have written this into our journal—today being Thursday for me—and me being you. I know what you're probably thinking because I'm you, and well. . .this is a little difficult to explain, but I'll try to explain in a way that would be believable to me, being you, and you, being me.

I am you, Khepri, writing to you two days ahead of you. You should receive this message on Tuesday night around 10:45pm, shortly after returning from drinks with Mark and Laura. You are getting ready to write a letter to yourself, two days into the future. To me.

To verify that this is not a hoax and that you are not going crazy, I am to provide you with the name of our second grade teacher, or something like that. Interestingly enough, I cant remember their name at all. There is a fog over those memories, and you would know that about us already.

You may be wondering how and why you are receiving this letter, if you have received it. I am intercepting your communication with me, two days in your future because I believe that something has gone wrong with the experiments.

I knew something was off two days ago, on Tuesday, where you are now. I went into the office for work, talked to Mark about ETO, and at 9:45, I received the message in Outview telling me to read ahead to Chapter 2. Except, I should not have been the one receiving that message. I should have been the one sending it. Leaving me to wonder, who sent it, if I didn't.

Ever since, I had been feeling strange, like this intense feeling of unfamiliarity with my surroundings...not exactly lost...but when I, for example, walked into the office - a space that I walk into many times a day and don't think twice about it – there was this temporary delay in time and recognition of where I am, momentarily disassociated from myself. Then I catch up with myself to experience that very instant in time, if that makes sense....Of course it doesn't make sense. I'm not sure if you are experiencing the same, but if you are, you will empathize with my loss for words to explain this. It's almost like... reverse déjà vu (which is actually called jamais vu – I thought I'd save you the trouble of looking it up).

I am not quite sure what is happening. My mind...our mind?...is playing tricks. And at this point I feel like we should probably continue reading ETO in order to reassemble the pieces. But I think it's time we took a little bit of control and found a more efficient means of communication.

Assuming normal rules of cause and effect are intact, I thought of a method that will hopefully resolve any paradoxes that would result from our out-of-time communication.

Every Friday afternoon, we sit down in the library to transcribe our interviews for that week, right? There was nothing else on the schedule for this week, but Mark is going to schedule you an interview tomorrow. After you finish the interview, record a message for me letting me know that you received this letter. When Friday comes and I go to the library to transcribe, I will hear your message. This will confirm that we are able to communicate without use of ETO and the exercises.

Let's see if this works.

Love,
Me (future you)

She sat on her bed and read the entry so many times that the words checked themselves into her memory banks.

After what seemed like the thousandth read, she finally got up, and walked slowly, nervously into the bathroom. Keeping the lights off in fear that she would encounter a broken piece of her self, waiting there in the mirror, Khepri fished around in the bathroom cabinet until her hands came across a small cylinder.

Old habits die hard.

She gulped down two of the tiny round pills with a glass of *Pinot Grigio* as a numbing agent, and then passed out on the couch in her living room, falling into a thick, dense dream of nothingness that felt familiar, even comforting.

The present contains nothing more than the
past, and what is found in the effect was
already in the cause – Henri Bergson

The laws of nature are just that—laws, and as such, have all
of the features of laws. Convenient, interpretive, a static
container meant to apply to dynamic sets of circumstances,
created and defined by those in power, influenced by the
institutions of politics, economics, and society.

Laws of nature are formed from observations of relationships
between phenomena, and then justified by repeat empirical
studies. As you prune away at any particular law to try to
find its underlying justification, you will ultimately arrive at a
set of axioms—axioms that were also derived from
observational regularities. Although we can prove a statement
to true by deriving it from axioms, we cannot prove the
axioms themselves.

Either we must accept certain axioms as true and factual starting points, or we must prove the axiom. And base axioms do not offer inherent proof. The axioms observed in nature are not nature itself, but rather "nature as exposed to our method of questioning," (Heisenberg).

Thermodynamics is an example of a law of physics that has reigned over the modern-day understanding of chaos, time, and has held humanity in the static grips of a linear progression of time.

The principles of thermodynamics, despite not actually applying to the dynamic set of circumstances in which time and forms of matter may present itself, nonetheless are a widely accepted explanation of the composition and direction of matter. And, like laws governing human behavior, it is looked upon as "illegal" in the field of science (and in the everyday experiences of reality) to challenge or break these laws.

The laws of thermodynamics are essentially specific manifestations of the law of the conservation of energy. Internal energy of a system:

Law #1 (Conservation)- Energy can neither be created nor destroyed, but can only change from one form to another, thus the total amount of energy and matter in the Universe remain constant.

Law #2 (Entropy)- In all energy exchanges, the potential energy of the system will always be less than that of the initial state; if no energy enters or leaves the system.

The beginnings of classical thermodynamics tie it intimately to the industrial revolution. Systematically developed around 1824, thermodynamics was advanced by mechanical engineers trying to improve the efficiency of steam engines during the Napoleonic wars of France.

The developers of the science had little concern with the meta- and micro- physics underlying the substances which they were studying.
Rudolf Clausius, one of the major developers of the theory, purposely kept ontological beliefs (the study of the nature of being, existence of reality) about the motion of heat particles separate from his theories on thermodynamics because he did not want to "taint the latter with the speculative character of the former."

One thing that is not often noted in general discussions of entropy and other thermodynamics principles is that its proof is only statistical in nature, as it applies to large systems or "macrostates." On the microscopic (or quantum) level, the motion of matter and particles does not have an arrow of time (time indeterminate). The arrow of time is generated when we observe and measure the particles.

(society – time in mass. Does not apply for individual, subjective perceptions of time and order. Validity in terms of describing a system [or proscribing a system])

The subjective sense of time that an individual experiences, is oft determined within the brain by the thermodynamic principle. As Stephen Hawking noted in A Brief History of Time, disorder only appears to increase with time because we measure time in the direction in which disorder increases. This is circular reasoning, disorder being defined and measured by the very concept that it defines and measures.

How is a closed system defined?
Tradition and prejudice.
Double slit experiment.

Cause and Effect

Hawking says that our subjective sense of time is determined within the brain by the thermodynamic arrow of time, which is entropy. However, this does not hold true for all states. A later state of even an isolated system can be of lower entropy than an earlier state—melting ice, for example. What we base the arrow of time on, entropy, is actually only statistical in nature, not a hard and fast rule, as we take it.

"We should remember that while the causal continuity picture may account for any ordinarily observed event or series of events, it cannot explain the serial distribution of events in general. It can only account for a particular series within a perspective which assumes the fact of sequentiality and the validity of certain fundamental series of events. "

The concept of cause is based upon intentional acts from an agent/actor.[12] The agent uses the cause to bring about the intended effect. Simple example is that I am hot and I get up to open the window to catch a breeze.

---

[12] "THE FUTURE EXISTS

FIRST IN IMAGINATION,

THEN IN WILL,

THEN IN REALITY" – Wilson, p. 259

The cause here is wrapped up with my intentions, and the effect, wrapped up in the act, is the fulfillment of those intentions. According to ordinary perception, the act performed (opening the window)is brought about by the intention of the agent (me wanting to catch a breeze). Cause/effect and intention/act are present.

Now, let's make the example slightly more complicated by reversing cause and effect, so that the effect becomes the cause of the action.

Reaching back, the breeze from the window that my *self* desires to experience is the cause of me getting up to open the window in the first place. The future act/effect here (opening the window, getting a breeze) determined the state of which it was to be a natural consequence, its counterpart cause/intention (being hot, opening the window).

Forward Cause and Effect:
I am hot > *I will open a window* > I feel a breeze

Reversed Cause and Effect:
I feel a breeze < *I will open a window* < I am hot

You can also see how things overlap in the middle, where the act is concerned. Where they overlap, is where intention matters.

Determinism that takes cause/effect and effect/cause as equally possible and probable. If the conscious state is in free-flowing, dynamic existence, it can move forward, back, circle, spiral, or take on any patter or shape of choosing, depending on the observer and his intentions. But it must exist, it cannot not exist. When we live or relive or predict future moments, we are simply drawing from and freezing (assigning a fixed shape and flow to) the conscious state.

We craft it to fit our aims/intentions, or we craft it automatically based on past psychic states that have built up patterns in our minds. These conscious states do not otherwise need to be named or expressed, for they are constantly acting, actualizing, and coming into being. But we freeze, label, and name them for the purpose of communication.

At point X, the conscious state looked like X------. At point Y, it looks like Y------. Remove time/space points, you get free flowing conscious states that blend to create one being. Insert time/space (measurement) you get shape, definition, association, pattern, contrast

The act is never done, it is a continuous and dynamic flow of events with dynamic possibilities, the well of which we choose from at any given moment and fixed point in time and space, crystallize and create experience (frozen)

Quantum Causality

".. subatomic events cannot be understood in Newtonian terms and must require some sort of acausality (indeterminism) or holism (super-determinism) to explain them. In either case, the distinction between 'observer' and 'observed' breaks down. Jung···had observed that···synchronicities, weird coincidences - tend to occur when certain deep structures in the psyche are activated. He assumed that these structures were at what he called the 'psychoid' level, below the collective unconscious, where mind and matter are not yet distinct - the quantum foam out of which matter and form and consciousness hierarchically the larger the scale of the object, the more classical causality will reign. Cause/effect collapses into binaries at the macro level.

At micro/quantum level - Causal order of events put into superposition (2 places at once). The order of events is indefinite until observed and collapsed (similar to the location of a particle). [13]

Wave function in a quantum system will follow all paths of possibility/probability until it is forced to choose a path (the act of observation). Once observed, it will follow the path of least resistance – quantum Darwinism. Quantum systems are "forced up" into a macro system following the path of quantum Darwinism upon measurement

Desired future determines the past. Past constantly being altered by future and vice versa. We are usually unaware or unaffected in the local present.

Some theorize that the causal effectiveness of our conserous intentions rests heavily upon the quantum zeno effect, and has been advanced as the dynamical feature that permits free choices on the part of an observer to influence his or her bodily behavior. The brain creates, in an essentially mechanical way based on trial and error learning, as well as the quantum state of the brain, a question. Each possible question is associated with a psychological projection into the future that specifies the brain's computed expectation about what the feedback from the query will be (Sapp, p 7)

---

[13] "scientists from UNIGE's Faculty of Science were able to entangle two fiber optics populated by 500 photons, unlike those that were previously entangled to only one photon. To do this, the team led by Nicolas Gisin, professor in the Physics Section, created an entanglement between two fiber optics on a microscopic level before moving it to the macroscopic level. The entangled state survived the transition to a larger-scale world and the phenomenon could even be observed with the traditional means of detection, i.e. practically with the naked eye. In order to verify that the entanglement survived in the macroscopic world, the physicists reconverted the phenomenon at the microscopic level." - What if quantum physics worked on a macroscopic level?   **http://m.phys.org/news/2013-07-quantum-physics-macroscopic.html**

Interference patterns form when two realities/possibilities are simultaneously valid.

- "A single looping path back in time, a time spiral of sorts, behaving according to Deutsch's model... would have to allow for a particle entering the loop to remain the same each time it passed through a particular point in time. In other words, the particle would need to maintain self-consistency as it looped back in time. In some sense, this already allows for copying of the particle's data at many different points in space," Wilde said, "because you are sending the particle back many times. It's like you have multiple versions of the particle available at the same time. You can then attempt to read out more copies of the particle, but the thing is, if you try to do so as the particle loops back in time, then you change the past." To be consistent with Deutsch's model, which holds that you can only change the past as long as you can do it in a self-consistent manner, Wilde and colleagues had to come up with a solution that would allow for a looping curve back in time, and copying of quantum data based on a time traveling particle, without disturbing the past. "That was the major breakthrough, to figure out what could happen at the beginning of this time loop to enable us to effectively read out many copies of the data without disturbing the past," Wilde said. "It just worked." - Time warp: Researchers show possibility of cloning quantum information from the past http://m.phys.org/news/2013-12-warp-possibility-cloning-quantum.html

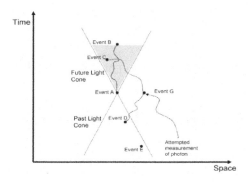

Experiments

1. How do you know that you, as a person and as an identity, exist across time and space? Find a childhood picture, around the age of 3 or 4. Try to get inside the moment you took the picture. See if you can transport yourself back there. Can you remember the moment before the picture was taken? What about the moment after? The moment of? What were you thinking? Get back inside your own head. If you are unable to do carry out this exercise, think about why. Are you really the same person in that picture?

2. Can you cooperate with your self in the future to download a future memory? This requires communicating with a future self to pass you back information. Both sides must work together, and trust each other.

WEDNESDAY
Crystal Quantum Memory

*"Whatever is a reality today, whatever you
touch and believe in and that seems real for you
today, is going to be - like the reality of yesterday
- an illusion tomorrow.*

    -   *Luigi Pirandello*

Khepri should not have been surprised, but still was,
when she walked into the office Wednesday morning. Mark
told her that he had worked his magic and managed to get
Khepri an interview that day with Ms. Alberta Johnson, the
mother of thirteen-year-old Jaden Johnson, recently locked
up in *Haverford Juvenile* for murder. The interview was
scheduled for that afternoon at the teen's house, around the
corner from where the murder had taken place.

Jaden's story, despite being unusually violent for such
a young child, had been nothing more than a blurb in the
Metro and a forty-five second feature on the nightly news.
When put into the context of the *Haverford Experiments*,
however, the details of Jaden's crime and background
perfectly fit the pattern of Khepri's story; a Black adolescent,
involved in a violent crime, with no history of violent
behavior, with the crime taking place in North Philly,
adjudicated to *Haverford Juvenile.*

Authorities were still uncertain as to where the gun came from. Jaden had been walking to the corner store to get a snack after school. A few witnesses to the crime stated he was standing outside the door dressed in all black, with a hoodie over his head.

When two young men walked out of the store, Jaden shot one of them in the stomach. There was no apparent motive— no robbery attempts. The little bit of news she could find on it offered no further details.

Although she was all too grateful to spend the day out in the field and not focused on ETO after what happened last night, it seemed that she could not escape the weird. As she did some brief research before the interview with Ms. Johnson, more uncanny connections began to present themselves in the *Haverford Experiments* story, too.

Like other details of her youth that had faded or been repressed through some form or another, Khepri couldn't remember very much about her time at Parallel University. What she could remember was that as a foster care youth, she had been a part of a pre-college prep program that DHS offered; allowing her to survey a few courses of her choosing for a few weeks during one summer when she was thirteen or fourteen. She was allowed to stay on campus in the dorms, like a real college student. The program was housed at Parallel U. the summer she was in it.

After she cross-referenced the initials in the memo to the names of faculty and staff of the school, she found two possibilities for the D.H. initials noted in the memo their informant passed them from Haverford Juvenile: a Dr. Diop Hammond of the Psychology department and a Professor Dennis Humphries of the Biology Department. Either guy could have been the one, so she printed out both men's profiles.

After reading Dr. Hammond's profile and seeing his picture at the end of it, Khepri was immediately gripped by an unsettling memory of him. He was one of the professors who taught some of the courses she surveyed, back when she was in the college program.

The coincidence was too much for her to ignore. He had to be connected to the *Haverford Experiments*. More poking around on his department's website yielded a large database of research articles, studies, and experiments that Dr. Hammond had been involved in. She printed out a few of them and skimmed for anything bearing a connection to the *Haverford Experiments* and the pattern of behaviors exhibited by the boys involved.

One article in particular stood out to her. It was a research study involving a neurological machine that Dr. Hammond had invented called the psycho-temporal transcranial stimulation device, or the PTSD. The article said that the PTSD was used to stimulate areas of the brain responsible for memory and time perception. Although the device was said to have therapeutic aims, one small note in the article mentioned that it could possibly alter behavior.

Once she saw the picture of the device, she felt certain that this was the thing being used on the boys. The image alone made her uneasy. It looked a lot like a dentist chair, a monitor attached where the dentist tray would sit, and a helmet that resembled the hood of a hair dryer.

However, the article was from 2002. She thought that, given the updates in technology, it could be easy to dress the machine up to look less clinical and imposing and more like a modern day arcade or virtual reality game.

She made some notes on the article; but, before she could read it at length, it was time for the interview with Ms. Johnson.

***

When she arrived at the Blumberg Housing Projects later that day, Ms. Johnson came to the screen door smoking a cigarette.

"Who you? DHS?" she called out from behind the screen. In between shadows cast by a muted mid-day sun, Khepri caught snatches of a dark-brown, middle-aged woman with thinning black hair.

"No ma'am, I am not. I'm from the newspaper, *Sun-Times Journal*. Khepri Livingston. You spoke with Mark Bloom about me coming to talk to you about Jaden?"

"Oh yeah, another reporter. Come in." She walked away from the screen door without opening it for Khepri.

Khepri stepped into a tiny, but clean living room that opened up into a kitchen. The room had all the basic furniture—an entertainment system, couch, coffee table—but it was obvious the mother was making do with what she had in dismal circumstances. Behind the furniture, Khepri could see peeling paint and cracks spidering up the walls. Beneath her feet, a shabby brown carpet receded back from the edges of the room. Bars on the windows painted a dark art of lines and space upon every object standing in the path of light streaming in from outside.

As Ms. Johnson led Khepri into the kitchen, she looked back at her with a scowl, expecting to see the look of disgust or discomfort that she had seen on the faces of the other reporters. But Khepri disappointed her. The surroundings, though unpleasant, were too familiar to the young reporter, if anything, being a close approximation to the many homes she'd lived in through her childhood.

After Ms. Johnson grumpily gave her consent to be recorded, Khepri set up the digital recorder on the kitchen table between them. She noticed, as she was setting it up, that the recorder showed a file saved and dated for today. Not sure of what it was, and not wanting to record over another interview she might have saved previously, Khepri pressed play on the file and heard herself give her usual opening spiel: introducing herself, stating the date and time of the interview. "Khepri Livingston interviewing Alberta Johnson on Wednesday, March 23, 2014 at 12:10pm..."

The date and time given in the recording was *now*. Khepri fumbled around hurriedly for the stop button, before anything else could be said, pressed it and created a new file. Ms. Johnson gave her a funny look, and then rolled her eyes at Khepri from across the table.

After she finished fiddling around with the recorder, she pulled out a paper and pen while talking, giving an identical opening spiel to the one that she had just heard moments ago; and launched into some preliminary questions about the Johnson family. She then asked the mother openly about how Jaden became involved in such a horrible crime.

"Well, it all started when these people from Parallel University or whatever it is. They came here back around August of last year, and told me they wanted my youngest boy to go to the school for some interviews and tests."

"Did they ever explain to you what kinds of tests and interviews?"

Ms. Johnson seemed to get a little defensive with the question. "Nah, not really. I mean, they said it was safe and everything. They said he was just playing some video games and taking intelligence tests. All the paperwork said they just wanted to see what kinds of effects video games had on kids, stuff like that. I didn't see nothing wrong with that. He plays videogames all the time." She pointed over to the x-box.

"He does? Do you mind if I take a look?"

Ms. Johnson rolled her eyes and nodded. "Yeah, and I keep all my paperwork, too. I still have the form I signed."

"Great, that will actually be really helpful. I would like to see that as well, when you get a chance." Khepri looked through the games. There wasn't anything unusually violent, like *Grand Theft Auto* or *Call of Duty*. There was some sort of ninja fighting game. But the rest of the games were sports or educational. She had seen more violent games on open display at toy stores.

"Who were the people who came to talk to you from Parallel University?" Khepri asked.

"Some blonde-haired little white thing came to do the recruiting. Seemed like she couldn't stand being around here, but she tried to grin and bear it. I saw right through her act."

"Did they offer you any money or gifts or anything for participating?"

"Yeah. They gave me $100 every time he went."

"Wait, I thought you said it was a one-time thing?"

Ms. Johnson frowned. "No, you never heard that come out of my mouth."

Khepri apologized and made notes in her pad. The fact that the experiments had taken place over multiple sessions seemed like more evidence that it could be connected to the PTSD machine and research she had just read about.

"Well look, just for the record or whatever. I wasn't just tryna collect a paycheck. I *do* have a job."

"I understand that, Ms. Johnson. I'm not judging you. Honestly, who couldn't use an extra $100 right now?" Khepri said. The mother seemed to relax slightly, taking a deep puff on her cigarette before continuing.

"At first I didn't understand how they had found my name, or how they knew I had a twelve year old son. When I had asked them, they said random selection from school records or something. That didn't make any sense to me, because I know that stuff is supposed to be private or whatever," she explained.

"But later I put two and two together. My older boy, James, he's up at *Haverford* for two years. Got caught stealing some change out of unlocked cars. He told me they had made him take the same tests and play the same games as his baby brother. I guess whatever they did didn't take on him," the mother said.

"Why do you say that, Ms. Johnson?"

"Well, because Jaden is younger, you know? He's more. . .uh, whats that word? Impressionable. He's more impressionable than James."

"And how old is James?" Khepri asked.

"He'll be be 18 next month."

What Ms. Johnson said sounded accurate. The experiments were likely to have had a greater effect on Jaden, than James. Khepri had done some background research on adolescent brain and cognitive development. The effects of an experiment on a teen, especially one involving the brain, would be strongest earlier in adolescence when the child's hormonal levels are highly variable and characterized by rapid fluctuations. Effects would decrease later on in adolescence as levels stabilize.

"The experiments were done on both James and Jaden," Khepri said, scribbling furiously on her pad. "When did you find out that they did the tests on James too?"

"Well, it wasn't until after Jaden got arrested. James said they weren't supposed to tell anybody about the tests, otherwise, they would get longer sentences. And they told him his sentence might be lowered if he participated."

Khepri was appalled by the fact that James had received placement in a juvenile detention center; taken away from his family and school for two years, for stealing some change out of cars. She suspected that James was also a victim of the "new deal": trumped up sentences for petty crimes being imposed on youth, in exchange for kickbacks from private kid prisons like *Haverford*. It was happening all over Pennsylvania, most notably in the Luzerne County "cash for kids" scandal.

But Khepri decided to stay with her original line of questioning, and not probe too much until she had established more rapport with Ms. Johnson. The mother was on edge as it was. *And rightfully so.*

"So what did James and Jaden tell you about the tests and the games they were playing?"

The mother tensed up again, a dark look flashing across her face. "Jaden can't really remember much. My baby's in some kind of shock. But James, he told me that he didn't really feel like himself when he was inside that thing, playing it."

He said it was like being inside someone else's mind. His thoughts didn't feel like his own, and he couldn't move the way he wanted to."

"How did the game work?" Khepri asked.

"He got in some chair and was strapped in, with some helmet on their head, and some little things attached to their skin, like little head phones or something. James says the scenes in the game were kind of like *Grand Theft Auto,* or whatever its called, but in North Philly. The game had North Philly streets, and people we know from the projects. He said he almost thought he was out of jail and back home, he couldn't tell the difference," Ms. Johnson said.

Khepri shivered as she listened to the woman's account of her sons' description of the game.

"And what was the goal of the game?"

"This is the crazy part, Miss. James says the goal of the game was to kill as many people as you could. You also gotta sell drugs to get points. If you do things like rob people, and break into stores without getting caught, you get more points."

"So did you begin to notice any changes in Jaden's behavior after he started participating in the experiment?"

"Yeah, I'd say after three or four sessions, something changed about him. He just seemed so agitated all the time. . .and always keeping secrets. He's always been my baby, up underneath me everywhere I go. After the sessions, he started spending a lot of time in his room and being mean to his brothers and sisters. Then his grades started slipping and he wasn't wanting to go to school."

"I see. What made you decide to come forward now?"

"I'm not just coming forward *now!* I told the cops, I told the judge, I told them dumb ass reporters that came around here before— tryna get a juicy story out of me. Everybody says it's open and shut.

And I told them, like I just told you. My boy has never been violent a day in his life, until after he started going to those sessions at Parallel University. He wouldn't have hurt a roach. And he's just a baby," Ms. Johnson said.

Khepri believed the mother, but she wasn't really sure how to tell her that, because it *did* all sound so crazy. But her own experiences over the last few days were beginning to expose just how thin the line between reality and fiction was.

So instead, she just listened to Ms. Johnson. She felt that was more important than finding the right words right now – letting her get her story out without interruption or judgment.

"Look. I know it may look like I live in a hell hole in here. . . around me. . .but I love my children, and I try my best. We mind our business. I go to work, my kids go to school, and we come home. My older boy got caught stealing, but he was just. . .he wanted something he couldn't afford, and he didn't understand that wasn't the best way. You grow up in a place like this, sometimes you can't see a future for yourself, other than what's around you."

"But my youngest, my baby, my little Jaden. He is just a baby and he wouldna ever did this if somebody hadn't put him up to it! That little boy was going to get us out of here!" Ms. Johnson said, tears welling up in the corner of her eyes.

But she never let them fall. Khepri admired her strength.

"I understand more than you know, Ms. Johnson. More than *I* may even know." Khepri finally offered. "Someone took advantage of you and a lot of other families. A lot of lives have been destroyed."

She couldn't look the mother in the eyes when she said, "I promise I will get to the bottom of this."

She didn't want to simply be another person full of empty promises for her. She wrapped the interview up and thanked Alberta Johnson again.

***

The memories did not begin to flood her all at once. They came in like trickles through the cracks of a dam. A piece floated by as she got back inside her car after the interview... a flash of Diop Hammond standing over top of her.

Another came, as she made her way back to her office. This one struck her so hard and so long that she had to pull off to the side of the road. Her hands were shaking so badly she could not control the wheel properly. In the memory, she was strapped into a chair, tubes in her arms and hands. She felt the tiny shocks of electrical pulses running around on her scalp like little bugs.

Her brain was trying to communicate a message to her body that her mind would not accept.

That she had not been at Parallel University, taking pre-college level courses.

She had been at Parallel University as part of the first clinical trials of the very machine that was being used in the *Haverford Experiments*. Khepri had been experimented on at Parallel University when she was fourteen, just like the boys at *Haverford*.

And someone, or *something*, had suppressed her memories of it.

After several heavy inhales and exhales, she resumed driving to the office. She began wondering why, if Khepri two days in the future had had this same interview and been led to the same realizations, she had not mentioned it in her letter to Khepri last night in the journal.

Either it had not dawned on her that they were more deeply involved in all of this then they could have ever imagined, or she had purposely omitted the fact.

Both scenarios were scary. Khepri's consciousness had not only split along past, present, and future, it seemed the *future her* now embodied a consciousness of *her own*. The future Khepri seemed to be, in some odd sense, a whole other individual. One with whom she shared memories with, had some shared past and common identity; but with her own intentions, motivations, and decision-making agency. There seemed to be no clearly defined *I* here: they were both *I* among their isolated selves, dynamic in their own rights within their discrete moments in time.

On the other hand, future Khepri still seemed bound to the same general events on the same timeline. She, for example, had had the same interview on Wednesday that she later told Khepri about.

It seemed in the natural order of cause and effect, that *she* could affect future Khepri's timeline, but not the reverse. The very idea that there could be a *future self* existing independently of her—that this self could make contact with or that could affect her environment— assaulted Khepri's experiences of cause and effect.

Even if cause and effect could be manipulated, as their communication and ETO suggested, the world around her still adhered to the classic rules. Fighting against them was essentially like fighting gravity. Humans couldn't fly no matter how hard they swiped at the air.

Their experiments with time had found some way to bend the rules, or create variables within her local environment. Either that, or they had "collapsed" into a universe where all scenarios were possible: entanglement and relativity were in operation simultaneously.

She figured that the *future Khepri,* who she had started calling *K2* in her mind, and herself as *K1,* would be sitting down Friday transcribing the interview from this afternoon, in the *Sun Times Journal* library. And K2 would be expecting a message from her. She usually transcribed in the library at six PM on Fridays, when the building was a little quieter.

In her, *K1's now,* it was only one PM on Wednesday. This gave Khepri five hours to figure out how to play this with K2, and see how she could get more information from her. The fact that K2 was expecting to receive a message from past K1, and wasn't sure if she would get it or not, told K1 that her future self did not completely control the flow of information.

For the next few hours she sat at her favorite desk in the corner of the library; positioned in front of a large window overlooking the city skyline and surrounded on both sides by shelves, with her back turned to the other researchers in the library. Headphones on, she combed through articles on time travel, and philosophy of mind and consciousness. She emerged from the corner only for bathroom breaks, food, and the occasional incensed phone call from Mark, who wondered when she was bringing her ass back to the office.

She took notes, read quotes, sketched diagrams and graphs in her notebook, and plotted coordinates of time, space, and depth until she felt she had finally devised an experiment of her own, without making her future self aware of what she was doing in the past:

Prior to our intermingling, our existence in the "classical" universe looked like this:

$$Pk \vdash \sim Nk; \ Nk \vdash \sim Fk; \ Fk \vdash \sim Pk \quad [14]$$

---

[14]

<u>Key:</u>

P = Present	K = Khepri & = and
N= Now	$\vdash$ = "entails"
F = Future	$\sim$ = "not"

Past Khepri does not entail **Now** Khepri. **Now** Khepri does not entail **Future** Khepri. **Future** Khepri does not entail Past *Khepri.*

Nothing intermingled. Each Khepri was in the **Now** *relative to our position, existing in our own classical universe bubble, and the Now contained neither the Future nor the Past Khepri. In communicating through the ETO experiments, we collapsed our "individual" space-time lines to look like:*

Pk & Nk & Fk

Past Khepri and Now Khepri and Future Khepri.

Every instance of Khepri contains all three positions of past, present, and future - there is no discrimination.

K1 and K2 have some measure of free will in our relative space-time locations, but are connected by a common timeline/moving along the same temporal line.

Writing it all out did the trick in helping her to generate ideas. One idea struck her as relatively easy to try out, a technique she used all of the time when she had nightmares or a bout of sleep paralysis. Astral projection. She could do something called an *ultrashort projection:* a quick exit of and re-entry into her physical body. She didn't want to stay any longer than ten seconds or so, to avoid cluing K2 into her presence; or worse, getting stuck in K2 and not being able to return to her own physical body. She couldn't even conceive of what that would mean for her in her present, here in Wednesday.

Khepri had never tried astral projection in a waking state, but she had trained herself well enough to project-at-will whenever she was having an uncomfortable sleep paralysis experience.

With what I'm coming to understand about time and space, through what I'm experiencing and reading in ETO, it shouldn't be that hard to apply the techniques in the waking reality. It seemed at least worth a calculated risk if she could get in and out of K2's head quickly.

K2 would be coming upstairs in ten minutes to sit down at the same desk there on Friday; and would have on headphones to do the transcription of the interview with Ms. Johnson.

Khepri needed to use the next ten minutes to put herself into as deep a mental trance state as she could go. She slipped her own headphones on to muffle out any excess noise coming from the library around her. She then tried to quiet her mind of any thoughts that did not consist of her present environment. . . her body. . .her self. She then extended those thoughts to her self, two days in the future; she tried to recreate the feelings and sensations she imagined herself to be experiencing two days into the future, all while pulling the image of K2 into her mind very vividly. In a few seconds, she felt herself actually there in the room, two days in the future.

At first K1's conscious awareness hovered over K2's body, who sat at the desk, with her head phones on, fumbling around with the recorder. But like a vacuum sucking up dirt, the conscious awareness is pulled down into K2, and K1 is now inside of K2, as if it were her own body (although, technically it is her body). She can see herself and can actually physically feel herself picking up her tape recorder, rewinding back, and pressing record. K2 is getting ready to record a message that will show up on K1's tape before Wednesday's interview, affecting the past, so that when K1 went to transcribe on Friday, she would hear it.

But then she interrupts her own thoughts. K1 feels K2's mind change and start down a different path of thoughts. *Hey, I feel you in there!,* she thinks to herself...

Khepri became disoriented, pulling back out of the future memory. Confused, for several moments, she couldn't tell if she was still in Friday—inside K2's head—or back in Wednesday. She looked down at her clothes to see what she was wearing. The outfit quickly confirmed that she was, in fact, back in Wednesday.

She took a deep breath of relief. But she realized the breath had been taken too soon, when she noticed that her tape recorder was blinking red. It had a new recording on it.

Khepri pushed play to hear the new message, and her own annoyed voice spilled out of the tape.

It was K2. "So that was *pretty uncomfortable,* but it was interesting. I like how you tried it. I guess you don't fully comprehend yet that nothing gets by me, here, in the future? It's called entanglement, Khepri. I guess we glazed over that lesson in ETO, huh? We are like two entangled particles. Anything you do in your environment will cause some sort of change or fluctuation in my environment immediately, and vice versa."

"It's not like, butterfly effect entangled, though. It seems like the universe won't fluctuate that much if only minor changes are made." K2 said.

She continued, "At any rate, I knew something was up because I went back and checked. On *my* Wednesday afternoon, right after the interview, I sent myself a blank email. You know, laying the path. Today I went to check the email around one PM, and that email was nowhere to be found. Not in my inbox. Not in my deleted box. It's not a surefire thing; but, all other things being equal, you should have sent out a similar email. I should have had two emails. Or the one that I sent should have still been in my inbox. Neither of those scenarios occurred. That confirms that you are not strictly adhering to my timeline. Maybe 98.9%. I still basically know everything you are going to do before you do it. But that 1.1% can cause a lot of trouble, apparently."

At points throughout the recording, Khepri almost didn't recognize her own voice. It sounded like her. Yet there was something else, a bitter undertone, that she had never heard herself use. It made her heart pound a few paces quicker.

"Personally, I think it's not worth fighting over and trying to one up each other. That won't end well for either of us." K2 said. "What we want to do is exploit this. Use it, *double team and co-exist*. Imagine how much more efficiently we could gather information? It's like quantum computing. Both of us feel like we have something at stake here, with this split consciousness we're sharing. Plus, the weird temporal disorders and *jamais vu* we keep having are only going to increase if we don't figure out how to make this work.

So listen, I have an idea. I think you. . .*we*. . .were on the right track with the whole astral projection, focusing forward thing."

Khepri heard K2 pause and flip some pages in the background. "I diagrammed this out. We need to get to a point where we can be in the same room, so to speak. Where we are sitting right now is a good place to meet up. It's a sort of neutral zone, versus being in our apartment around all of those objects and personal memories, confusing things. We are going to create a series of memory-moments here in the library that we can then project ourselves into and meet up.

I'm going to start tonight, Friday. I will sit here from eleven PM tonight until it is midnight, Saturday. Tomorrow, on Saturday at eleven PM, I will do the same—sit here until midnight on Sunday. Sunday night, I will be here again," K2 said.

"You will repeat my actions *exactly*. When you reach Friday, sit in the same exact spot, from eleven PM to midnight, as I will have already done. At precisely twelve AM Saturday, you will project your consciousness twenty-four

116

hours into the future, into a memory of twelve AM Sunday, which I will have created. It will be Sunday going into Monday for me."

"At precisely twelve AM, I will focus my consciousness into the memory I created, in the library, twenty hours into the past: Saturday going into midnight Sunday. We will meet there, as two individual consciousnesses in one physical space on Saturday passing into twelve AM Sunday."

"Now look, the memories have to be very *specific*. You must be wearing exactly what I will be wearing. Your actions must mimic my own. We will also listen to the same song during that hour, because the music should help make the memory stronger. If all goes well, we should meet in the middle at exactly twelve midnight on Sunday. And Khep. . .don't do anything I wouldn't do. Got it? I swear I know how to destroy you if I need to," K2 ended the message.

Incredibly distressed by K2's message, Khepri put the tape recorder down and her head down on her arms with it. She didn't know what to do next. All she could think was to return to ETO for guidance.

Experimental Time Order

Chapter 4

"A time traveler, like anyone else, is a streak through the manifold of space-time, a whole composed of stages located at various times and places. But he is not a streak like other streaks. If he travels toward the past, he is a zigzag streak, doubling back on himself. If he travels toward the future, he is a stretched-out streak. And if he travels either way instantaneously, so that there are no intermediate stages between the stage that departs and the stage that arrives and his journey has zero duration, then he is a broken streak." —David Lewis

As human beings traveling along the line of time, we perceive that we do not have immediate access to experiences of the past or experiences of the future. With the past lying behind us, and the future always moments, days, months, or years ahead, we are essentially resigned to experiencing the sensations of the immediate present. As a general rule, human consciousness can only focus on what it can see, smell, hear, or feel in its immediate environment.

Despite this being the general rule, however, human consciousness comes equipped with its own set of tools known as memory and imagination, which function to manipulate the rules of the present senses. Memories (which can be triggered by a particular smell, a noise), can temporarily displace our focus onto something that we experienced in the past. Imagining, envisioning, or daydreaming the future allows us to anticipate what may come, and, if we follow along the path of our visions, we may even arrive upon the future that we imagined for ourselves.

<u>Memory:</u> when does an event or experience become the perceived *past,* is it after one second has passed? And when it does pass, how do we go about retrieving that past experience? **Memory is the first thing that comes to mind. It allows us to** conjure up an image, a pocket of time that we temporarily displace my senses in. Think sort of the reverse of a black hole, where time is created, instead of stripped away into its basic element.

"Is it the perception which determines mechanically the appearance of memories, or is the memories which spontaneously go to meet the perceptions?" —Henri Bergson

When we time travel into the past, we must necessarily time travel into memory, unless we accept that some objective camera (God eye?)(light?) is recording every moment; because something must account for all the perspectives that converge to create one event. You must take into account the relative perspective of every object in the room giving the scene its depth. For example, "When the mind naturally reviews memories from slightly different perspectives. . .it is spontaneously engaged in constructing alternate realities. This spontaneous construction of alternate realities has survival value in a constantly changing environment."[15]

---

[15] Mind and nature are in constant change and creative flux. It is irritating to us when our memories of the same event are different from those of another person, and when even our memories change over time...The law requires that a witness repeat the same story in the same way every time. The natural mind, by contrast, tends to repeat the same story, with variations, seemingly seeking to constantly update and reframe "reality" in keeping with the new information and views it is spontaneously generating." — (Rossi, New Language of Mind-Body Communication, p.69)

The event must be accessible and subject to being re-created. "Memory does not operate like a tape recorder in which we simply play back exactly what we learned. Memory is always a constructive process whereby we actually synthesize a new subjective experience every time we recall a past event."[16] This makes time travel impossible in a deterministic, classical universe. If all events are recorded, stored up and waiting to be arrived into, that means you can't travel to that event unless you're traveling into that event was part of the event in the first place (see *grandfather paradox*). It would take an infinite amount of energy for a body to physically go back to some specified time, date, and location[17]. How could that location possibly still physically exist? It takes infinite amount of energy to physically maintain every moment— and what is storing those moments? They would need to be layered on top of each other, superimposed, like a quantum computer; or like memories in a brain.

Thus, you can't physically, as a massive body, by a classical physics definition, travel back! But as a quantum body, or a holographic body, you can travel back effectively via memory.

---

[16] Rossi, p. 69

[17]"Pure information, in the mathematical sense, does not require energy; it is that which orders energy. It is the negative of entropy, that which brings disorder to energy systems." — Wilson, p. 246

Memory, like light, wraps itself around all objects in a room. Each object and item is recording the space-time event from its own perspective. In order to reconstruct a space-time event, you would have to get the memory from each object to build up the scene. Like a Scavenger hunt.

The other possibility is that events can be altered but only within a small degree. The other perspective is that every decision made splits into multiple universes in which case you may travel from universe to universe, posing no effect on the universe from which you have traveled.

Quantum Decoherence – the larger a quantum system gets, the more it interacts with its surrounding environment, which in turn decreases its quantum properties.

Can we change our destinies? There is perhaps a combination of fate and free will, a concept that is neither one or the other and simultaneously both. Metaphorically, it is like the wave/particle duality of light. Or, like Shrondinger's cat, in that it collapses into one or the other whenever we attempt to observe or influence the process.

There is at least an illusion of change, as there are illusions of time and illusions of space-solidity. But does that substance of change extend beyond the material, immediately perceivable world?

 Perhaps the illusion of change arises from the tensions of living confined to the dimensions of time and space. Because we are psychologically (ego) bound to time and space, and we believe that time moves forward, that we are in motion through space, change must exist. The ego cannot process stillness. . .so it creates motion, change, temporality of past/future to move back or forward into (past memory and future intention). Patience diminishes the tension between time and space by bringing together "that which time and space separates. . ."[18]

Patience is the gray area, a ground zero of sorts, where time and space converge to bring one to their destination, where they arrive at their intention. Destiny derives from the word destination, "a goal which is aimed at by each individual of his own free will." What we refer to as destiny is manifestation of intentions/reaching goals.

---

[18] Atwater, P. M. H. Future Memory. Charlottesville, VA: Hampton Roads Pub., 1999. Print.

Incubating Mind-Body Healing

1. Readiness signal for present problem review

    When your inner mind is ready to review all aspects of that problem as you are currently experiencing it [pause], you'll find yourself getting more comfortable and your eyes will close. [Pause] Review, especially, all parts of it you don't know how to deal with yet.

2. Incubating current and future healing

    Now explore the future healing possibilities. How do you see yourself? How do you feel? What are you doing now that the problem is completely healed? [Pause] Now let your inner mind review how you are going to get from the present problem [pause] to the future when you are healed. [pause] What are some of the steps you will take to facilitate your healing? [Pause]

3. Ratifying mind-body healing

    When your inner mind knows it can continue the healing process entirely on its own, and when your conscious mind knows it can cooperate with this healing [pause], you will find yourself stretching, opening your eyes, and feeling refreshed as you come fully alert.

The Psychobiology of Mind-Body Healing

We have access to our thoughts, but not its underlying process, only the byproduct, in word form. What lies behind thought? From where does it arise? How? Why? Word = Thought. . .are there no thoughts beyond words? What about thoughts that go unacknowledged, running beneath the stream of consciousness? Can they be called thoughts, too, if they do not arise in our present consciousness?

Does a thought only exist (by strict definition) if we are aware of it?

Words contribute to the perception of linear time, perhaps even create it, our sense of time logic. But words are only themselves abstractions of concepts begging for further definition. Bergson on the matter: *"We instinctively tend to solidify our impressions in order to express them in language...we confuse the feeling itself, which is in a perpetual state of becoming, with its permanent external object, and especially with the word that expresses the object."*

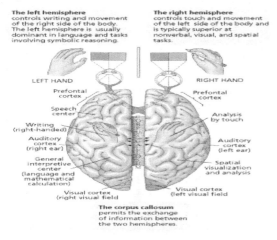

The left hemisphere controls writing and movement of the right side of the body. The left hemisphere is usually dominant in language and tasks involving symbolic reasoning.

The right hemisphere controls touch and movement of the left side of the body and is typically superior at nonverbal, visual, and spatial tasks.

LEFT HAND

RIGHT HAND

Prefontal cortex

Speech center

Writing (right-handed)

Auditory cortex (right ear)

General interpretive center (language and mathematical calculation)

Visual cortex (right visual field

Prefontal cortex

Analysis by touch

Auditory cortex (left ear)

Spatial visualization and analysis

Visual cortex (left visual field)

The corpus callosum permits the exchange of information between the two hemispheres.

One can not

usually make a claim that a word is original, only re-arranged and perhaps pre-arranged in time/space. However, context is ever-changing, dynamic, in a state of perpetual creation by each individual employing static words...so the action within words that create a context endows it with uniqueness in practical usage.

Dreams and Memory Why are dreams so difficult to recall upon waking up? [19]

It seems that memory is bound up in action. When dreaming, my body does not move, I lie still in bed. Because there is no bodily movement (no action while dreaming,) memories are not being recorded. In waking life, I can not recall the dream state because my body has not recorded the dream's actions. [20]

"You ask me what it is that I do when I dream? I will tell you what you do when you are awake. You take me, the me of dreams, me the totality of your past, and you force me, by making me smaller and smaller, to fit into the little circle that you trace around your present action. That is what it is to be awake. That is what it is to live the normal psychical life. It is to battle. It is to will. As for the dream, have you really any need that I should explain it? It is the state into which you naturally fall when you let yourself go, when you no longer have the power to concentrate yourself upon a single point, when you have ceased to will. . . ." – BergsonThe word "will" as Bergson uses it, takes on

---

[19] "Use the snooze button for short [astral] projections. This is also a handy way to get around some mind-split effects by limiting the time of a projection. Set your snooze button to gently wake you at ten- or fifteen-minute intervals. When the alarm goes off, hit the snooze button and attempt a quick projection, going straight to your projection technique each time…as soon as you remember something, write it down. It helps if you have the alarm clock, pen, and notebook within easy reach, so you will not have to disturb your relaxed too much while using them." –Bruce, Robert. *Astral Dynamics: The Complete Book of Out-of-body Experiences.* Charlottesville, VA: Hampton Roads Pub., 2009. Print., p.280

[20] "When the mind-split occurs, a full copy of consciousness and memory stays resident inside the physical/etheric body at all times. This, the original master copy, is fully capable of independent thinking if it has the energy and training to hold itself awake. But it normally becomes semi-conscious and falls asleep soon after the mind-split occurs." — Bruce, p.299

multiple significances with supreme equilibrium, (will as action/will as intent):

- **verb** (used with object), verb (used without object) to wish; desire; like: Go where you will. ask, if you will, who the owner is.

- **noun** 1. the faculty of conscious and especially of deliberate action; the power of control the mind has over its own actions: the freedom of the will. 2. the wish or purpose as carried out, or to be carried out: to work one's will.

- **auxiliary verb** 1. am (is, are, etc.) about or going to: I will be there tomorrow. She will see you at dinner.

- (in relevant part from **dictionary.com**)

Everything has intention attached to it. A beam of light knows where it is going before it gets there, and always chooses the shortest path to reach its intended position, meaning it already knows where it's going and how to get there before it even departs from its resting state.

With intention, there is a purpose in all of our acts and action— everything we do carries a particular purpose, to achieve a particular result, to arrive at a particular destination. The result that we wish to achieve is our desire, our goal, the thing toward which we direct our efforts, the fruit of our actions, what gives our actions any meaning or significance.

*"But let us sum up briefly the essential difference
which separates a dream from the waking state. In the
dream the same faculties are exercised as during
waking, but they are in a state of tension in the one
case, and of relaxation in the other. The dream
consists of the entire mental life minus the tension,
the effort and the bodily movement. We perceive still,
we remember still, we reason still. All this can abound
in the dream; for abundance, in the domain of the mind,
does not mean effort. What requires an effort is the
precision of adjustment. To connect the sound of a
barking dog with the memory of a crowd that murmurs and
shouts requires no effort. But in order that this sound
should be perceived as the barking of a dog, a positive
effort must be made. It is this force that the dreamer
lacks. It is by that, and by that alone, that he is
distinguished from the waking man."* — Bergson

Living involves a necessary sort of tension, difference,
distinction, discrimination, and a constant choice between
two states (by way of metaphor, the scientific theory behind
Schrodinger's Cat thought experiment explains the concept).

Experiments

1. *Attempt to test the dream/action/memory theory out by
monitoring your dreams. What types of dreams are
remembered best? Which ones create the strongest reactions?
How does background noise influence dreams? What senses
and sensations do you experience in dreams (sight, sound,
touch, smell, taste, time, temperature, direction, balance, pain,
and motion)*

2. *Recall a memory, then get inside of the memory to actually re-experience it. Not just a flash or an image, but build up the scene of the memory like a play set, and step onto the stage. Describe the memory from the perspective of the other objects in the room.*

3. *Observe your thoughts passing by and attempt to find the origin of thought, the well from which it springs.*

4. *Find patience, the space in between each thought, the gap from one thought to the next. Afterward, answer the following: Can you separate your self[1] from the thought of the thought? Can you separate your self from the experiment? IS there a moment between thoughts, where time breaks down? Does "a moment between" imply that there is "space" between thoughts? Can thoughts be said to exist in a space?*

5. *Pay particular attention to thoughts you have and order them in terms of their relation to the past, present, or future. For example, if you have a thought about something you plan to do tomorrow, order that into the future. If you have a memory of the past, order that into the past. If you have a present sensation, such as a thought about your current surroundings or a feeling of discomfort, place that thought into the present category.*

---

[21] "The real issue is to transcend the observed isolation of a self. A humble 'self' or surrender of the self, may constitute an opening of the focal setting to some small degree." – Tulku, Tarthang. Time, Space, and Knowledge: A New Vision of Reality. Emeryville, CA: Dharma Pub., 1977. Print.

6. As you categorize these thoughts, notice where you place the "future" thoughts, "past" thoughts, and "present" thoughts in your imagination. Are the past thoughts behind you and the future thoughts in front of you? Take a specific thought from either one of those categories and reverse the direction. If it is a past thought, for example, reverse the thought so that you see it in front of you. For a thought about the future, reverse it so that you see the thought behind you.

7. Take one of the future thoughts that you have reversed and build up a memory of it, just like you did for the past memory in exercise #1. Place your consciousness inside of the future memory to experience it.

8. Take one of the past memories that you have reversed and walk into it, as if it is unfamiliar. As if you are experiencing it for the first time.

THURSDAY
Beat Frequencies

"Water has a perfect memory, and is forever trying to get back to where it was."
—Toni Morrison

Beyond feeling fearful about K2's threats, by Thursday, Khepri was feeling increasingly drained and disoriented. She felt herself repeating conversations that she wasn't sure she hadn't already had— retracing steps she had already walked— just in case. Memories of past instances in time had her unable to distinguish between what was happening to her *now* and what she had done *before*. Just as K2 had experienced. Her disorientation made it unclear how to even begin protecting herself from K2.

She also now had to account for the immediate past. She was nervous that there was a past her, a K0, perhaps, following along the intermingled timeline. K2 had told her not to worry about it yet on the tape. But what if a Khepri in her past, a *K0*, had picked up *Experimental Time Order*, was doing the experiments, had made contact with a few other Khepris, had collapsed and intermingled other timelines?

Simultaneously, she had to participate in the common *present.* Mark would soon be expecting an extensive update on what she had found out about Parallel University, and at the interview with Ms. Johnson. She couldn't bear listening to the interview again right now, not after getting K2's message. Preoccupied with her rogue future self and ETO, she had not done much follow-up on *Parallel University.* Instead, her work bag was full of articles waiting to be read.

Part of her also knew that she was afraid of the memories snatching at her again, pushing her to face whatever had been buried in her past about *Parallel University.* She wished she could tap her heels three times and return to her normal, classical, Newtonian universe. She knew all the rules of the game there.

As the day wore on, she tried to calm her mind enough to push through the foggy moments. She knew she had to have at least as much information as K2 did, if not more, before they were to meet up. She didn't really trust K2 to do the right thing; especially knowing that K2 saw her as a disadvantage, since she existed in the past relative to K2's space-time.

For that reason, she wasn't sure if K2 wanted to meet to try to work together, or if she was looking to get rid of her past self all together, as she had threatened on the recording.

Yet, the more she thought about it, the more Khepri began to see that her disadvantage might also be manipulated to her advantage. K2's fear of the past left her with vulnerability. K2 was constantly trying to overcome K1 by using information that her past self did not yet have access to. K2 also had an obvious disdain for her, seeing K1 as behind her and not particularly useful.

Khepri knew that she had a bad memory. Always had. Being honest with herself, she had to admit that the memory was, in part, intentionally bad. She learned early on how to draw a curtain over the damaged parts of her life, how to bury painful memories and push herself into a state of traumatic amnesia.

And for this reason, she spent many years crafting a perfect, packaged timeline of success. The foster kid who made it out of sheer hard work and opportunity. But no one knew about the infinite moments before she got there— or *how* she got there. She made sure of that.

At the same time, nothing was ever entirely lost. A number perpetually divided into halves will never equal out to zero. Just because she had rendered those parts of her life invisible, did not mean they had disappeared.

K1 needed to use and manipulate past information, memories, life experiences in ways that she had never used them before. The things she spent her life running from, were the only things that could save her as she faced her most formidable enemy: *herself*. Her plan was to plant something in her past, carefully crafted to cause a major fluctuation that would keep her along the same basic path - but something K2 in the future wouldn't see coming.

After she got home from work, it was tempting to go into her spare room and start tearing open boxes, pulling out old journals or books or pictures, what little she had kept and carried with her or hadn't donated to a thrift store, in order to induce memories. However, she knew that a large enough action on her end, would trigger a reaction in the future-present that K2 was in. No, this needed to be psychological warfare.

Easing into a comfortable position on her living room couch, with the lights off and no music, Khepri closed her eyes, relaxed her body, and sunk herself into her past life, into places that had long been buried.

The first stop on the memory road map was seven years before, almost to the day. She was a student at Loyola University on scholarship in an advanced track Journalism program.

Khepri had struggled with suicidal thoughts all of her life.

But she had always found ways to compartmentalize the destructive urge. Or channel it into what she thought was a healthy exploration of things, like out-of-body and near-death experiences. On one occasion it had occurred to her to go see the free psychologist on campus, like all the other students did for their eating disorders and inabilities to focus without prescription drugs. But her first appointment filled her with more anxiety than the problems themselves.

Having to sit there and talk about her issues so intimately with a stranger, someone who was supposedly objective but who was, in all likelihood, in their head judging her the whole time. If journalism had taught her nothing else, it was that objectivity was an illusion, as was confidentiality. Besides, one appointment was all that she needed to get a prescription for anti-depressants, which she took for several months.

Khepri remembered the night vividly now, something she had pushed out of her mind for several years. Now she felt like she was in the same room with herself that night, a ghost watching from the door, reviewing her past self like a scene in a tragic play.

It was three days before her twenty-first birthday and it seemed that all things in the universe had conspired to create a horrible day for her. She had been working two jobs, aside from taking on a full course load, because the scholarship only covered her books and classes and not her living expenses.

Having no immediate family back home in Philadelphia, she was always forced to keep two jobs to make ends meet; and so her school work and social life usually suffered as a result. The deadline for the final paper, in a class that she needed to pass in order to pass on to her senior classes, was approaching in three weeks. Her professor had sent her an email earlier that day about reviewing her sources, and she had barely even started on it. Her girlfriend, and only close friend of two years, also decided to tell her that day, via e-mail, that she wanted to start "hanging out" with other people.

Feeling utterly dark and hopeless, she had come home after work that day, and pulled out the trunk in her closet full o f some old journals from childhood, and pulled open the pages brimming with all of her old wounds. She began ripping out the pages from the journals, reading them, crying on them, balling some of them up, ripping others into tiny shreds, in an attempt to destroy her past.

It was this scene that K1 relived *now*, from her memory back in the room again. . . *After ripping through most of my journal pages and pictures I see myself popping the Xanax pills in my mouth like chips, then chasing them down my throat with a river of wine. As I watch myself reading through the book, I remember my own life* now, *as the drug and wine induced fog seeps into my brain. The lights in the room are dim. . . intimidating shadows played across the walls, as Mary J. Blige crooned sadly from the stereo from her* My Life *album...*

About an hour after she overdosed, Khepri's roommate Ebony found her lying unconscious on her bedroom floor in their suite, sprawled out atop a pile of books and papers. If it weren't for the overturned, nearly empty prescription bottle that lay beside her as a companion, innocently blurting out her secrets, Ebony would have thought

Khepri had simply fallen out from exhaustion while writing her paper.

Khepri had lay in a minimally conscious state in the hospital for nearly two days, one level shy of a coma. On the morning of the third day, shortly after the rising sun had passed directly over the Earth's equator, she had fought her way through what seemed an eternal stretch of shimmery black space; occasionally broken up by surrealistic imagery of a Topsy-turvy world, and rejoined reality for better or worse.

K1 reviewed all of this in her mind's eye, then pulled back to the present and sat up in the couch. As she settled back into her present-tense state, she felt that she had been able to modulate the strength of the experience's influence on her memory. The rememberance had reverberated through all levels of her self-awareness, constructing an alternate reality where she could recognize and integrate what she had just witnessed in the past memory. For the first time in days, she felt confident that she had communicated with herself, was now more fully conscious of how her past was connected to her, still and always.

K1 had planted an important message to her self that night, 7 years ago, one that would reminder her that the past remains alive and that her actions, at all times, influenced both the past and future.

Experimental Time Order

Chapter 5

By a spark of the conscious, sound was light that split into language. letters spun, splashing together. Thought is synonym for memory. Take tense for its shape.

Sound can be used to store information and knowledge.[22] Music effectively acts like a time machine. It's like a vehicle through which I can be transported back to a certain place or event or moment efficiently and completely, because music is interwoven throughout the fabric of events that make up one's life. What lies behind that note, or that string of notes, what is contained within melodies and sounds, glued together to make a song, that has the power to

---

[22]"Like the strings on a violin or the pipes of an organ, the proteins in the human body vibrate in different patterns, scientists have long suspected. Now, a new study provides what researchers say is the first conclusive evidence that this is true. Using a technique they developed based on terahertz near-field microscopy, scientists from the University at Buffalo and Hauptman-Woodward Medical Research Institute (HWI) have for the first time observed in detail the vibrations of lysozyme, an antibacterial protein found in many animals.The team found that the vibrations, which were previously thought to dissipate quickly, actually persist in molecules like the "ringing of a bell," said UB physics professor Andrea Markelz, PhD, who led the study."via "The Symphony of Life, Revealed: New Imaging Technique Captures Vibrations of Proteins." **http://m.phys.org/news/2014-01-symphony-life-revealed-imaging-technique.html**

transport you back to that memory?[23] With music, everything is built into the present tense moment of your listening experience, much like how all objects are integrated into one visual frame as a seamless whole scene.[24] With music you do not have to anticipate the future, nor recall the past. It is one continuous flow, a never-ending present that is only split into future-past upon the observer's measurement.[25]

---

[23] "Musical time is not like clock time, or time as idealized by classical physics. Clock time is purely reiterative, a mere succession of isolated moments. Musical time is integrative of many moments." – Grandy, Everyday Quantum Reality

[24] "Sound at the atomic-scale has the same dual nature [as light], existing as both waves and quasi-particles known as phonons. Unlike elementary particles such as electrons and photons, whose wave nature and coherent properties are well-established, experimental demonstration of coherent wave-like properties of phonons has been limited. This is because phonons are not true particles, but the collective vibrations of atoms in a crystal lattice that can be quantized as if they were particles. Read more at: http://phys.org/news/2014-02-crossover-unambiguous-evidence-coherent-phonons.html#jCp" Light and sound are similar in various ways: they both can be thought of in terms of waves, and they both come in quantum mechanical units (photons in the case of light, and phonons in the case of sound). In addition, both light and sound can be produced as random collections of quanta (consider the light emitted by a light bulb) or orderly waves that travel in coordinated fashion (as is the case for laser light). Many physicists believed that the parallels imply that lasers should be as feasible with sound as they are with light. While low **frequency** sound in the range that humans can hear (up to 20 kilohertz) is easy to produce in either a random or orderly fashion, things get more difficult at the terahertz (trillions of hertz) frequencies that are the regime of potential phonon laser applications. The problem stems from the fact that sound travels much slower than light, which in turn means that the wavelength of sound is much shorter than light at a given frequency. Instead of resulting in orderly, coherent phonon lasers, miniscule structures that can produce terahertz sound tend to emit phonons randomly. Read more at: http://phys.org/news186059734.html#jCp

[25] "Not only is the past gathered into the flowing edge of music, but the future is as well. Again, we know this from everyday experience: while listening to music we feel stretched out towards a happy resolution, a return to the home key. And as musical tones integrate past and future to produce musical wholes, they trigger within the listener an expansive and heightened sense of the present moment." – David Grandy

Sound and vibration phenomena resonate, literally and figuratively, with the living body. All matter, including physical bodies, is made up of "interacting electromagnetic fields vibrating at tremendous frequencies." And remember, "the broader our frequency response, the larger the number of realities in which we can function."[26]

"Scientists have known for a while that ultrasonic waves can affect cells in many ways. For instance, physicians use ultrasound to stimulate the production of blood vessels and bone; it's also used in heat therapy. When applied to neurons, ultrasonic waves can change how the neurons generate and transmit electrical signals. A new model may help clarify much of this behavior. This new way of understanding the interaction of **sound waves** and cells relies on the **cellular membrane**...[a] microscopic structure in the skin that surrounds a cell, keeping the organelles – like the nucleus and the DNA it contains – in, and the rest of the world out.

The molecules that form the membrane are arranged in such a way that there are two layers, with a space between them. According to Kimmel's model, when the ultrasonic waves encounter a cell, the two layers of the cellular membrane begin to vibrate (much like how a person's vocal cords vibrate when air passes through the larynx). Cell membranes also act as capacitors, storing electrical charge. As the layers vibrate, the membrane's electrical charge also moves, creating an alternating current that leads to a charge accumulation. The longer the vibrations continue,

---

[26] Bentov, Itzhak. *Stalking the Wild Pendulum: On the Mechanics of Consciousness.* New York: E.P. Dutton, 1977. Print.

the more charge builds up in the membrane. Eventually, enough charge builds up that an action potential is created."[27]

Matter	Rate of Vibration (at room temp)
Atom Nucleus	10^{15} HZ
Atoms	10^9
Live cells	10^3

"Our bodies are oscillators, and the atoms making up our bodies are also oscillators. Therefore, we expand into a space-like dimension many times a second rapidly and collapse back as rapidly, possibly at the rate of atomic vibration." – Bentov

7Hz rate of motion/pulsation is the trigger rate for "ejection" from the body[28]

When matter vibrates, it is blinking in/out on/off action/rest

yes/no 0/1

---

[27] Unlocking the Brain's Secrets Using Sound, phys.org
http://phys.org/news/2014-01-brain-secrets.html#jCp

[28] "It has been known since the famous experiments of Heinrich Hertz near the end of the 19th century that light is a wave consisting of electric and magnetic fields, just as radio waves and microwaves. The only difference is in the number of times these fields change their direction in a second." Via Light oscillations become visible http://phys.org/news977.html#jCp

In order for matter to build up, it binds itself into larger masses with lower vibration rates.

Rest = infinitely fast motion

Rest is made of motion. Motion arises from rest. A point of rest in a pendulum swing must be reached through a period of motion. Motion is achieved through the build-up of infinite moments of rest. Where rest and motion reconcile, matter obtains physicality...or perhaps it is the tension between rest and motion that creates physicality

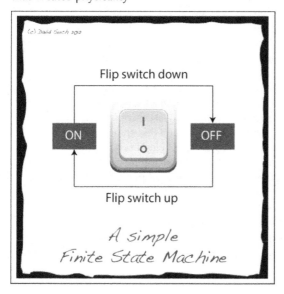

A simple
Finite State Machine

On = motion inside the rest state ...in constant oscillation

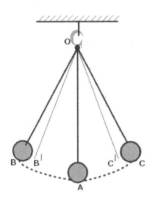

Our whole sensory system operates this way, whether it is optical input coming through the eyes, acoustical through the ears or tactile through the skin – and the end result is a series of spikes conducted to the appropriate area of the brain. In short, our senses translate the surrounding reality to us into a Morse code language of *action and rest*. Action comes when the neuron fires its spike, and rest comes as the cell is regenerating and readying itself for the next firing. Out of this action and rest code our brain constructs for us, for example, the form of a rose, its texture, its color and smell – in other words, its "rosiness." Or it will construct for us a faint image of distant galaxies coming in through the eyepiece of a telescope. – Itzhak Bentov

"Whereas a classical bit of information either takes on the value '0' or '1', quantum particles can be placed in superposition, meaning they can be either '0', '1' or '0' and '1' simultaneously. These quantum bits enable powerful new ways to process information. They are, however, also extremely vulnerable to errors, such as accidental flips from '0' to '1' or changes in the phase of a superposition. Even the tiniest of such errors continuously accumulate to inevitably erase the quantum information. It is therefore crucial to timely detect and correct errors…The theoretical solution, found in the nineties, is based on entanglement. This is the counterintuitive phenomenon that quantum systems can become so strongly connected that they can no longer be described separately. By encoding the quantum state in an entangled state of multiple quantum bits it is possible to compare the states of the quantum bits to detect errors, without measuring or disturbing the encoded quantum state itself."

> "We could compare solid matter to ice and mind or consciousness to steam or vapor, all being the same basic stuff in different form. Both of them are manifest only because they are changing, and this change can be measured against the basic sea of the absolute, which makes up both the ripples and the background. We don't need to wonder now about feats of mind over matter it is not so much mind "over" matter as mind "over: a different aspect of itself." – Itzhak Bentov

It seems that Change silently threads itself through experiences, slowly and surely winding itself so tightly so as to become embedded in events, giving an observer the appearance of having always been there. The change is so seamless, has assimilated itself so precisely that it may go virtually unnoticed. It is only when you later tread into your memories to re-examine and reflect; it is only when you turn the light on time and gaze upon the past and remember what it is that you asked for, do you realize that the change is already underway and it is in the now.

The change has infected your interactions with your external world, thus affecting the feedback you get from those interactions, and the responses that those interactions trigger within, a circular flow. The change-infested waters of the circular flow spins new worlds into motion, rich with their own possibilities, mirror reflections rendered unto themselves. You are allowed to choose amongst them all. In this way, change does not override that which already exists within, but instead, it coexists, running parallel at points with an individual track, and intersecting at other points, blending into a whole.

The changes are like the seasons in the sense that summer turns to fall, fall turns to winter, winter transforms into spring, and spring eventually becomes summer again. The seasons change and have differences and distinctions, on the one hand. But embedded in that very change is a permanence in that they must always cycle and overlap - these four seasons will steadily transform and change back into each other over and over again.

Then, within each season are these characteristics - we call it weather. The spring is characterized by light winds on some days, rain showers on others, growing from chilly to warmer and warmer as it progresses. Each season has a choice of which of its characteristics it wishes to display on any particular day.

At some point, you become aware of having more choices and modes of be-ing then those that you had before the change took residence within you. Though you can still choose to respond to things or people in the ways that you always have, you become aware that you are free to choose this change and to respond in the ways that has been integrated into your palette. It is stored away in your infinite, all dimensional hologram, and you now have access to those dimensions. You now realize that the hologram is within you and is you, and always was.

Change cancels itself out in some contradictory fashion, change itself is unable to change what it is, its own nature. By its name alone, it is constant, despite its perceived effective action. And a thing only becomes a change if considered, examined, defined, and named. Otherwise, it is just there, existing, acting, revolving, flowing. Movement is not in objects. Objects are movement, infinite vibration.

Transforming a Problem into a Creative Function

1. Accessing and amplifying a problem-encoded resource

   Access the circumstances during which a chronic problem becomes manifest. Gradually amplify your sensitivity to milder instances of the problem before it causes your usual discomfort. Wonder how your new sensitivity can become a resource for problem solving.

2. Transducing a problem into a creative function

   Use your heightened sensitivity as a radar to scan the minimal cues in the situations that are evoking your "problem." See, hear, feel, intuit the meanings of your mind-body responses. Record, draw, and meditate on dreams and fantasies about the problem. Recognize what personal developmental changes are needed for a wader adaptation to life stressors.

3. Ratifying your new creative function

   Review and contrast your old, painful, and maladaptive way of being with your new understanding. Reframe your previous life problems in the light of your new relationship to the world and self-identify that you are actively creating each day.

The Psychobiology of Mind-Body Healing

Experiments

1. Continue your experiments with time distortion. Sit comfortably in a seated position with a clock or watch in front of you. Stare at the clock as you relax your mind and body. After you feel completely relaxed, close your eyes and visualize an activity, such as completing a goal, with intense anticipation. Experience the thing you are visualizing completely, and with all of your senses. When you have achieved that feeling completely, open your eyes and look at the clock again. Do the hands on the clock pause or stick in certain places? After practicing this exercise a few times, you should be able to slow down or stop time consistently and for longer periods, as you experience a slower brain wave output.

2. Test your ability to slow time over periods of 10 seconds. Find a phrase to repeat (such as "I am" or "Time is slowing down" or "Time is speeding up"), and repeat the phrase over and over at the same pace over ten seconds. Count how many times you can say the phrase when you are focusing on distorting (slowing or speeding) time, and count how many times you can say the phrase when you are not focusing in a time distorted manner.

FRIDAY | SATURDAY

Time Loop Logic

*Let's look more closely at the nature of events as we
encounter them. Generally the focus-personality's [the
self we know in relation to exterior events] experience
involves specific space-time events, but as
precognition shows, some events are perceived in an
out-of-time context. Such an event still won't exist for
the perceiver as an ordinary [event]. A future
development "seen" now will still happen in the
future, and not at the time of perception. For
example, if A sees a vision in which B dies on a certain
future date, and if this probable event does
occur, then it will happen on the future date and not
in the now of the perception. For the perceiver, the
event may seem to happen twice; but when it does, it
will be in its own space-time intersection. . .A sudden
shift in focus conceivably could result in someone's
experiencing yesterday in everyone else's today. – Jane
Roberts*

Khepri woke up on Friday morning feeling not much
different than she had been all week. In fact, she felt *weaker*.
For all her remembering and planting last night, it seemed
nothing had changed in her immediate present— at least
nothing she could tell yet. ETO was still next to her on the
nightstand. A reminder that she was still stuck in this
fractured reality.

Mark was in her face for an update as soon as she
stepped into the office. She had already rehearsed an update
to him; one that didn't include telling him that she had likely
been experimented on by Dr. Hammond, at Parallel
University. Mark was probably the closest thing to a friend
she had; and yet she knew he was about his business first.

149

He would definitely question her bias and would feel the need to discuss it with Sharpe. This would inevitably lead to someone at the *Sun Times* being tasked with digging deeper into her past, beyond her resume, references, and recommendations. She would then be made a part of her own story, inevitably losing control over it, if not removed from it altogether.

And there was no way she could let that happen. This story was both bigger than her and it *was* her. Yet, it seemed inevitable that her connection would come out. If she planned to expose Hammond, she had to maintain control over the information at all times, something K2 had inadvertently taught her.

She gave Mark a synopsis of the interview, but did not reveal that she had learned any further information about Dr. Hammond or that she knew exactly what was being used in the *Haverford Experiments*. He gave her a mini tongue lashing for not having made more progress; but seemed temporarily appeased after she promised him that she would "hole herself up" in the library all weekend to dig up dirt on Parallel U.

That wasn't all together a lie. She *would* be in the library all weekend.

Khepri had seized upon another idea as a backup plan for dealing with K2. A footnote in ETO had briefly touched upon the concept of infinite regression, a concept demonstrated and refuted by a set of well-known thought experiments called *Zeno's Paradoxes*[29].

Zeno's Paradoxes stood for the proposition that movement can become impossible if the distance of the movement is recursively divided into smaller and smaller pieces. She had googled the theory for further information, and a series of hyperlink jumps brought her to the concept of *Thompson's Lamp*, a modern day variation of *Zeno's Paradoxes*.

There was a lamp sitting on the desk in the library where she was to meet K2. Her idea was to use the clicking on/off of the lamp to cut time into smaller and smaller slices, working to slow down time enough so that she would enter K2's memory of Saturday: twelve AM, a few seconds before K2 projected herself back into that memory.

It was the only way she could get ahead of K2, and hopefully lock her into a relative past. She didn't know if it would get rid of K2 all together, but it would at least put her in a better position to observe K2, and keep K2 from controlling her. Or worse, destroying her.

---

[29]The story goes that Zeno was a student of ancient Greek philosopher Parmenides, and that he created the Paradoxes as philosophical problems to support Parmenides's doctrine that motion is nothing but an illusion, that change is therefore impossible, reality is one, and existence is timeless, uniform, and unchanging, contrary to our senses.

At eleven-forty-five PM, K1 headed up to the office library and sat at the designated spot. She was grateful to be the only person there, besides one other straggler, which wasn't surprising on a Friday night.

She pulled on her headphones and pressed play on her CD player to begin looping the song that K2 had instructed them to listen to, *Melting Clocks* by Black Privilege. As the seconds[30] hand coasted past the twelve mark on her wristwatch, the minute hand crept slowly and dropped down onto the fifty-eighth minute line, Khepri flipped the switch of the lamp to *on*.

> *"I saw you walking down the plank*
> *Tiptoeing on the tightrope of time's hands*
> *When it became too inconvenient..."*

At eleven-fifty-nine PM exactly, she flicked the switch to *off*.

> *"Did you slip? Or were you pushed?*
> *There was no trace of blood*
> *There was no evidence*
> *And they won't ever know*

[30]

Time	State
0.000	On
1.000	Off
1.500	On
1.750	Off
1.875	On
...	...
2.000	?

And I won't ever tell
We share the same thoughts
On the clock stroke
Minds meeting at the crossroads
And there's nothing we can do about it."

Half a minute past eleven-fifty-nine, she flicked the switch *on*.

"We share the same thoughts
On the clock stroke
Minds meeting at the crossroads
And there's nothing we can do. . ."

She waited for the watch to move a quarter of a minute before she turned it *off* again.

"Seems like we're on the same wave
How many thoughts, I cannot say. . ."

At the next eighth of a minute, she turned it *on* again, and in exactly half that time, she flicks the switch back *off*. In exactly half that time, she flicked it back on.

In the next moment as the second hand inched forward she flicked the switch[31] her body felt paralyzed: frozen

---

[31]Then the question whether the lamp is on or off... is the question: What is the sum of the infinite divergent sequence +1, −1, +1, ...?" - James F. Thomson, philosopher and creator of Thomson's Lamp, a variation of Zeno's Paradox.

into one moment that she sensed was shifting into the moment before but without movement. . . for as time began moving forward she sensed that space was temporarily stuck and impotent.

Her eyes were fastened on the face of the watch as she witnessed the unfolding of the temporal-spatial order, the time reading twelve. When she began focusing forward on the memory of her sitting in the library twenty-four hours into the future, she felt her brain map the image of the second hand, on the first dash, in the next moment in a millisecond, divided by five million space and moved *backward*.

Her brain integrated the next image of the hand, inching back toward 11:59:59. Her perception of time-space coincided in the next moment as the second hand reached the fifty-ninth tiny dash on the watch's face.

> *"Slippin' off the ledge, slippin' off the ledge*
> *We're slippin' of the ledge, slippin' off the ledge*
> *I felt us slipping off the ledge of consciousness*
> *I felt us slipping off the ledge of consciousness*
> *I feel us. . ."*

Khepri was overcome by a sense of vertigo, as if she was falling, tumbling down into a blurry, spiraling tunnel of black space, encountering no resistance.

The mantle of her consciousness gave way like wax paper walls and she felt her self slipping, slipping through cracks that had colors she didn't know the name of. . . She may have been falling forever, she couldn't tell, but eventually she came upon a blank, empty, buzzing room filled with rippling walls. She landed.

She was out of her head now—her ego had evaporated. And though she knew herself to be connected to some physical body named *Khepri*, she felt she was both *Khepri* and *more than Khepri*. She didn't have to choose between, either, she could be both of and above.

The air in the space is alive and crackling with a palpable presence in the room. Light baths the space and she cannot see through her eyes. . . but soon her vision adjusts so that she is seeing without needing to look. Information about where she is, and who she is, and what is happening in the environment around her, is coming at her from all directions. She is absorbing it all without having to do anything. She simply knows, with no lapse in time, and understands what she knows.

She is now inside a moment of nothingness, at the point where time and space meet and created an intersecting line. Visible beneath the bath of light, and the grid pervading the space, is a pattern of the library she was just sitting in; in some shadowy form of reality.

There is no solidity to anything inside the room. Including the floor. Nothing has volume. Yet none of the objects in the room are falling through into the brightly-lit void that stretched out beyond the transparent confines of the room.

Set against the holographic backdrop of the library is a grid spreading out in all directions, connecting at the corners to create a cubed, gridded room.

Multiple layers of consciousness working separately but inter-meshed sticking like Velcro separating again, hooking together, working separately, but inter-meshed, dividing into multiple layers of consciousness.

They stand up, they turn around.

Khepri sees her self *standing behind her, who turns around simultaneously to see her* self *standing behind her. She walks toward her* self, *moving one square forward on the grid, as her* self *moves forward one square.*

They know what they are thinking before the thought arises *who am I are you we I am you are me we are me are you am I you are I am.*

She moves one square backward on the grid. As she moves back one square, walking away from her self. *I turn around to see my* self *standing in front of her. . . who turns around simultaneously to see her standing in front of her multiple layers of consciousness. Working separately, but inter-meshed, spring up against each other hooking together sticking like Velcro. . . un-pulling again. . . separating back into multiple layers of consciousness working separately but intertwined.*

She closes her eyes. . .

SUNDAY
Recurrence Plot

*A Recurrence Plot (RP) in chaos theory is a plot
showing, for any given moment in time, the
times at which a phase space trajectory visits
roughly the same area in the phase space.
Poincare's Recurrence theorem states that a
system having a finite amount of energy,
confined to a finite spatial volume, will,
eventually, return to an arbitrarily small
neighborhood of its initial state. The Poincaré
recurrence time is the length of time elapsed
until the recurrence. The result applies to
physical systems in which energy is conserved.
– Wikipedia*

Khepri could see and hear everything. The clock on
the nightstand next to the bed displaying eleven forty-four PM
in digital red. Quick movements flashing on the TV screen
across from her bed. The mechanical laughter of the audience
on a rerun of *Good Times*.

Slivers of pale light from the crescent moon were
slinking between the blinds through the window above the
dresser. Her ears were even picking up on the buzz of electric
energy that lay underneath the layers of noise and silence.
All of these sensations were cloaked with eerie shadows and
forms that daylight would normally mask.

Khepri was lying flat on her back in her bed. Although
she could not move her physical head, her torso, or any of her
limbs, all of her senses were intact, heightened even. She
should have only been able to see the ceiling from the position

157

she was stuck in, but her entire bedroom was squarely in a 360 degree view. On top of that, she was pretty sure that her eyes were closed.

It was happening again.

As Khepri surfaced out of the dream, she could immediately feel her real body tense up and get stuck. She was having another attack of sleep paralysis.

This particular episode of sleep paralysis was stronger and longer than her usual. She could usually count backwards from ten and snap herself out of the state. But this time, seconds seemed to stretch into minutes, as Khepri played tug of war with *dreaming* and *waking,* attempting to squeeze her body out of its immobility and back into the waking world. Although she felt time pass, the clock stayed stuck on eleven fifty-four, as if it would only move if her body moved with it.

Her thoughts, the only moving part of her, scrambled to figure out what to do next. She thought of some astral projection techniques, and tried releasing her astral body. Every time she tried to separate from her physical body, something or *someone* grabbed at her and pulled her back down into the frozen state, so that she was stuck in between, beating up against the walls of her own paralyzed flesh.

She counted backward from ten to one over and over again, hoping that the counting would animate the clock: t*en. . .nine. . . eight. . .seven. . .six. . .* and then she began panicking. *. .five. . .four. . . three . . .two. . .*

On *one,* Khepri shook herself awake with such a powerful shudder that she nearly fell out of her bed.

Back in the waking world, she was sweating and her blankets were twisted around her legs as though she had been kicking and thrashing in her sleep. She looked at her clock. Eleven forty-four. Her twenty-eighth birthday was in sixteen minutes.

What a way to kick it off. *Right on time, Saturn Return. Right. On. Time,* she thought sarcastically.

From outside the window the moon glowed tauntingly, bathing the bedroom in an eerie blue-gray light, unnerving her further.

Khepri grabbed her dream journal off the night stand, wanting to record the sleep paralysis experience, the failed astral projection, and the dream preceding both while it was all still vivid. The details were already beginning to leak out of her short-term memory bank.

When she picked up the pen to write she noticed that the last entry, which she had written a few weeks ago, spanned a few pages. It was quickly but neatly written and began on the left side of the page, covering both sides of the pages in the journal, like a letter. This was unusual to her typical entries, which were short, choppy, scribbled sentences in an effort to get down as many details about her dreams as quickly as possible.

She began to shrug it off and turn to a fresh page, when the date and time of the entry caught her by the eye, causing her fingers to freeze in mid-turn.

March twenty-second? What the hell is this?

With an eerie feeling creeping up the base of her spine, she spread the book open on her lap and began reading the entry. Her heart knocked harder at her chest as she recognized that the entry was a letter to herself, dated two days from now, and penned in her own heavy, slanted handwriting.

THE CONVENTION

(Deenah)

"Moments never last, and yet, there is always one present. Listen, there's a philosopher named Henri Bergson, late 1800s French guy. He distinguished between two types of memories. Memory Type One records the events of our daily lives as they occur in time, assigning a place and a date to each event on our personal timelines. When we want to recall these past moments, we imagine it in our minds, pull it out of our mental filing cabinets so to speak. The imaging of that event, the reconstruction of those recorded images in our mind during memory recall, is what Bergson calls the intellectual recognition of a perception that has already been experienced. These memories are vague, tinted with emotion, subject to our own personal fictions that conform to our worldviews."

- *Dr. Diop Hammond*

"I *said:* can I help you, miss?"

Deenah Lumari blinked at the bellhop standing before her. How long had she been standing here? Better yet, *how* had she gotten here?

Just a moment ago she was sitting in the driver's seat of her car in the parking lot. Now she stood at the lobby doors of the *Walton Hotel.* She distinctly remembered looking at the clock on her dashboard, noting that it was 11:55 AM as she turned off the ignition, feeling anxious about missing even a second of the lecture.

Then. . . *blank.*

She couldn't remember getting out of her car, grabbing her purse (which she now gripped tightly in her fist), walking through the parking lot, arriving here.

"Oh, I, uh. . .I'm here for the convention," she managed to stammer.

"Memory Type 2, however, is of a mechanical nature. We employ mechanical memory with every movement we make, in our repetitive actions, in every moment. Remembering to breathe without being conscious of the need, knowing how to put one foot in front of the other when we walk, without having to think about that process as we walk. Reading words without needing to recall learning how to read, that sort of thing.

This memory type—I call it the integrated memory—is dynamic because the memory is constantly in a process of creation at the same time that the memory is being utilized. Our bodies are taking in new information from the environment every moment and crystallizing it into memory. The body then uses the memories in a feedback loop, much like a cassette tape, to move us through time and space and into the future. And all of this action occurs before we are even conscious of it in thought."

Still feeling a bit disoriented, Deenah mused further about the blank spot in her memory as she moved through the near-deserted hotel lobby, past the concierge, into the Berkeley Ballroom and up to the convention registration table.

A pimply-faced, plump, and bespectacled man-child sat behind the table, dozing uncomfortably in a metal folding chair.

Her, "Excuse me," jolted him out of his dream. "Registration for PsychCon, please," she said feeling a touch impatient.

His flat gray eyes widened. "*You're* here for PsychCon?" he asked with poorly disguised sarcasm. He studied her freshly twisted dread-locs and rich earth-toned skin as if she were an alien, signaling a simultaneous intrigue and disgust with her body.

"Of course!" she said sharply, her words slicing the air.

His question seemed like a masked implication that she somehow did not belong here. An implication that she vehemently resented.

163

She'd often encountered these reactions at science conventions, expos, comic cons, and cos cons from jerks, just like this one, who couldn't believe that someone like her would be interested in such things.

Most of them tried to hide their surprise. Or, perhaps, thinking of themselves as progressives, were unconscious of their own biases. She would catch a twitch in the eye, a crack in the voice, or a feigned smile whenever she stepped into the room. Some of them ignored her presence altogether. Or she would be subjected to questions they would never ask of their white male peers, having to provide proof that she, a woman— and a Black one at that— was an authentic nerd.

But this particular registrant was treating her like an outright invader. He sniffed. "That'll be thirty bucks."

"I'm pre-paid. Deenah Lumari."

Deenah held out her hand to receive the name-tag that he plucked out of a stack nearby. But, as if her hand was made of an invisible substance, he completely ignored it; nearly throwing the name-tag across the table toward her.

Locking his cold eyes into an icy stare of her own, a split- second decision arrived now. Should she morph into the angry Black woman character he'd likely already assigned to her, or keep it moving?

She glanced at her watch, felt her heartbeat slow down and synchronize to the tick of the minute hand as it dropped into 11:59 AM, and took a breath for composure.

"Determinism does not defeat free will. They co-exist, like the wave-particle duality of light, or the liquid-solid nature of black holes, the electro-magnetic field, or any other number of binaries present in our physical reality. Choice has a duality—free will and destiny. It depends upon the observer, all of it. Unless you act consciously (free will), the next moment will be determined by your integrated memory, memory type II (destiny). So you can either act consciously to create the next moment or you will act automatically and allow stored, integrated memory to determine your next action."

Luckily for him, the watch had chosen her path. It was time to go. Besides, she was sure she would run into him again. They could finish this later.

"What room is the PTSD presentation in?" she asked.

But before he could answer—really, before the question even spilled out of her mouth—the room materialized in her mind's eye in *exact detail*. The room number on the plaque next to the door, a small crowd of people scattered around tables and chairs, a large object humped beneath a black sheet casting a deep shadow, and a man pacing back and forth before it.

Deenah thought she could even faintly hear speaking, though there was no one else in the Berkeley Ballroom except her and the rude registrant.

And, although she had never been to this particular hotel before, she felt sure that she knew *exactly* where the room was, and how to get to it. . . before the registrant lifted his beefy finger to point toward the elevator and mutter the room number.

Yet, the young woman was uneasy about how certain she was of the location, as if the knowledge was not hers to possess. The images of the room in her head were a patched-up snag in the fabric of her memory—like the memory wasn't there from something she herself experienced, and was instead stitched in.

Even as Deenah walked toward the elevators every step she took throbbed familiar, a dragging *déjà vu*. Along with the few seconds she apparently had lost getting from the parking lot to the hotel, the day had been strikingly peculiar so far. She wondered if she wasn't coming down with something.

The presentation was underway as Deenah slipped into the room. Just as in her vision moments ago in the lobby, the small crowd was spread out around tables, hushed with a hum of anxious energy.

What she assumed was the PTSD machine lay ominously in the background beneath a black curtain; Dr. Diop Hammond stood before it at the front of the room explaining the methodology of his research and the engineering behind the machine. Tall and thin with a short salt and pepper Afro and a slight Carribean accent, he occasionally waved his hands excitedly toward the black curtain.

"And then you see, by combining two notable brain stimulation techniques of transcranial direct current stimulation and transcranial magnetic stimulation, the psychotemporal transcranial stimulation device (PTSD) uses a noninvasive method to stimulate several targeted brain regions responsible for memory and time perception," Dr. Hammond said.

"The rest is all very technical, but you can read more about it in the materials I've handed out. The point is, by targeting regions of the brain responsible for short-term and long-term perceptions of time and memory, the first model of the PTSD allows the patient to 'functionally' relive not only their own memories with perfect clarity and consciousness, but also the memories of others, given the massive amounts of collected data that we have synthesized." Dr. Hammond paused for added effect.

"Based upon these essential theories, I submit to you that the *Psycho-temporal Transcranial Stimulation Device* is the world's first functional time machine," he announced to the audience.

The audience gasped and bustled and *oohed* and *ahhed*. Even after the discovery of faster-than-light neutrinos and the confirmation of the *Higgs-Boson Particle*, talk of time travel still belonged in the realm of the cautiously possible, but not yet probable.

One of the audience members said just as much: "That's ridiculous! Time travel isn't possible! For starters, it violates laws of causality and—!"

"And I will argue with you that it *is* possible, sir!" Hammond responded. "It holds up theoretically from any number of perspectives. Einstein's equations, for example—as any physicist will tell you—work just as well in whatever direction time is flowing.

The same equations that describe matter plunging to its death into a singularity at the center of a black hole, can be flipped to describe matter exploding from a singularity and spreading out through space-time to birth a universe! Time is but a feedback loop on the grandest scale, one that can be reversed or played forward. But before you cast your doubts, allow me to explain how it all works." Dr. Hammond pleaded, holding up his hands to tame the crowd.

Deenah had already read all of Dr. Hammond's published papers on the PTSD. Dr. Diop Hammond, a retired NSA analyst for the government, turned psychology professor, researcher, inventor, and lecturer, was a data expert. The key behind his theories was giving the brain direct access to collective memory.

For years, Hammond and his team of researchers at Parallel University had collected information from various databases on people and experiences—pictures, birth-dates, stories, videos, astrological birth charts, *Youtube* clips, diaries, statistics, research study results, and social networking profiles.

He then built a machine that used electromagnetic brain stimulation to access the collected data, building in algorithms to choose data and fill in any gaps in perception (memory's blind spots). The algorithms were as simple as the ones used by companies like *Netflix* to recommend movies to watch based on the subscriber's preferences.

The blind spots were filled in for lucid clarity of color, smell, sound, and all other sensory aspects of an experience or memory that were not normally re-experienced upon simply remembering a memory; and those particular smells or sounds that can function to bring a person back to a memory, like Proust's *Madeline Cake*. The body, under the control of the stimulated electrical brain impulses, could not tell the difference.

Dr. Hammond dramatically dropped the curtain under which the PTSD was hidden to reveal a seat attached to a monitor and a helmet connected to the machine via a coiled wire. The *"World's First Known Functional Time Machine"*, as Hammond referred to it, looked a lot like a high-tech version of the race car driving games found in malls across America. Below the monitor was a console with a number of unlabeled buttons spread out on its dashboard.

On either side of the seat, was an armrest with cuffs attached, resembling the blood pressure cuffs used in doctors' offices. The *traveler* would put the helmet on and be led into a semi-hypnotic state, with their heartbeat slowed to match a softly beeping timer. Dr. Hammond would proceed to guide the *traveler* through a lucid memory.

Dr. Hammond flipped through a Power Point presentation, which showed a diagram of the head and what parts of the brain were being activated with the PTSD. "When the brain simply thinks about action, the neural synapses are firing in the same cognitive and motor regions that they would if you actually performed the act."

"If you are being guided through a memory of a day at the beach in the PTSD, for example, not only will you feel the sand upon your skin and the screech of the seagull in your ear, but you will taste the salt water ocean on your tongue."

This was the part of the presentation that Deenah was most interested in. As a clinical therapist, she thought a device like the PTSD had potential therapeutic capabilities for her patients. As a general technology enthusiast, she was also interested in how the device functioned technically.

"And really, the stronger your connection to the memory, the more senses are engaged during the actual experience, and the better you will be able to relive the experience through memory. While in its current phase, the PTSD only allows you to remotely re-experience memories or events without influencing the environment of that event. With future models of the PTSD you will have the ability to interact with the environment, thus influencing the action," Hammond said.

"This will allow you to make a different decision that can affect your present reality. That's *right* people! You will be able to change the future or the past. Now some of you will continue to scream of these bloody grandfather paradoxes and free will and the like, and I will continue to defeat your logic with just one word: *intention,*" he told them.

Still, Deenah has her doubts about the PTSD, given what she had read. Raising her hand to interrupt ,she said: "Dr. Hammond, attempting to exploit the machine's therapeutic capabilities for recollection enhancement in cases of post-traumatic stress disorder, and attempting to progress research on the phenomenon known as post-traumatic slave syndrome, you've performed clinical trials of the PTSD on 100 participants."

"The trials have had varying results, with reported side effects ranging from skin irritation, nausea, headache, fainting, disorientation, minor cognitive changes, dizziness, itching under the electrode and, in extreme cases, seizures, psychiatric symptoms, and temporal disorders; in a rare but significant number of cases," she added.

Dr. Hammond squinted at her nametag before replying. "You've done your homework, Miss Lumari, very good. Many of the trial runs were inconclusive, investigative, or lacking substantive proof. And besides, with any new technology there are bound to be side effects. But, I assure you, it works safely on most participants, and it is achieves a level of contact with reality that a virtual-reality game could never touch! In fact, I'd say that temporal disorders are a desired effect of the PTSD," he said, chuckling lightly.

"To describe it best, the experience of sitting in the PTSD like peeking behind the curtain of your own consciousness, mid-thought, and discovering the wizard—which is you! Really, it is a chance to observe the feedback loop that keeps your conscious awareness functioning, as it is functioning. You get the opportunity to watch the play you are starring in from the audience, as you simultaneously play your role on stage, to parade back through your memory! Now, think of each scene in the play as a slice of time. . ."

Several hands shot up at once, while the man seated next to Deenah muttered beneath his breath, "I thought this was an emergent technologies in psychology convention, not a freakin' science fiction fair."

A confident man, Dr. Hammond anticipated the reaction of the crowd with an easy smile. "But you didn't just come here for talk, good people! Try it out for yourselves. As you all know, today's presentation is the PTSD's first public show and tell since the patent was approved. Per the terms of the authorization that you signed when registering for my workshop, I have fed the PTSD data of each pre-registered audience member."

"Along with an extensive profile on each audience member, we have linked the hotel's security cameras to the machine, and thus have looped recordings of each of you from the moment you walked into the building up until this presentation. That is what we will use as our demonstration memory. So, who wants to go first?"

"I will." Deenah jumped up, walked over, sat down in the seat in front of the console and slid the helmet on.

A live, real-time feed of her, sitting in the PTSD, flashed up on the monitor before her. She relaxed in the chair as instructed, reclining slightly, pulse slowing, the room around her fading into shadow as she stared at her reflection in the monitor, mirroring her actions in the chair.

Above her, Dr. Hammond's words fell softly into her ears and dissolved like snowflakes, "Close your eyes Deenah. You see, closing the eyes, immediately activates and enhances alpha wave and theta wave generation in our brains, which is connected to creatively sensing, feeling, and imaging. You are now facilitating a shift from the rational and linear processes of thinking to your more primary and holistic ways of thinking. Let's start off by recalling the moment right before this one...

Right as I say these words you are becoming conscious of how you are sitting. . .how you are breathing. . .where your hands are placed. . .listen to every word and become conscious of the word and the meaning. . ."

Deenah wasn't completely relaxed, and shifted uncomfortably in the chair as she felt a tingling in her head, like tiny bolts of electricity striking at her brain. It didn't hurt, but she was hyper-aware of the sensation, hyper-aware of her brain firing off synapses, hyper aware of one thought leading to the next. Her ears searched for something even slightly familiar, like the sound of Dr. Hammond's voice.

A clock in the corner of the screen counted backward from 12:15:09 PM. For blinking moments, she plunged in and out of an inky black. When she resurfaced, she realized that the scene on the monitor was playing in reverse from the time she sat down in the chair, to the time she entered the room. On the monitor, she would be back in the elevator soon.

"Now, in a quick succession of mental flashes, Deenah, recall and visualize everything you did from the moment you opened your eyes to wake this morning, up to this very moment, up to these very words that are coming out of my mouth. . ."

Her brain flashed the day through her mind as instructed, until it landed upon the image of her walking off the elevator into the lecture. Even though her brain knew she was still seated in the chair, she felt herself moving backward, as if she was walking too, mimicking her actions on the monitor.

Was she only thinking about the memory, or *is* she *there now,* walking through the lobby back toward the registration table?

"Remember, time flows differently for each of us, friends. Different strokes for different folks, or, as Einstein might put it, different rates of time relative to each person's perception. No two people see the world the same. You can bet, if I were to ask all of you to describe the hallway you had to walk through to get here, or to describe this very room that you are in, you all would have a different answer. Sure, there would be some overlay, but your perspective is uniquely situated in the world, colored by your attitudes, your emotional states, and your world experiences. And we have a way to recover those experiences—moment for moment, sensation for sensation, memory for memory. . ."

"Fuck, I'm gonna be *late!*" Deenah yelled, reading the clock on the dashboard: 11:55 AM.

Thankfully she was pre-paid for the convention. As she leaned over to grab her purse from the passenger seat, she became paralyzed by a curious sight just outside the car window.

She sat there in her seat. . . watching her *self* walking through the parking lot a few feet ahead of her car, puppet-like, as if being tugged by an invisible string.

Something was terribly wrong.

THE SHIFT

(Afina)

*"When the ordinary order of things are reversed, people often
cry out madness"*
– Luigi Pirandello

No one was really aware, at first, that *The Shift* had even occurred. Nobody started walking backwards, or anything like that. The fact that we are passing backwards into the seasons will offer no real indication either, since global warming has already made humans used to irregular weather patterns.

No, neither the human mind nor body handle change very well. At first, the mind-body, fearing what is unfamiliar, creates whatever illusion is necessary to ensure its survival, holds on for dear life to save its own skin, until its back is against the wall.

But in subtle ways, over time, apparently, whether it's unwinding or rewinding, change begins to work its way on both the body and the mind, oozing and setting into the cracks of things until reality presents itself to you as a smooth whole one day.

It is now November 7th, 2013, nearly two months into *The Shift,* and people are forgetting what used to be the future. What used to be the past - our already lived experiences and memories - grows hazier each day.

Past memories now only show up in the world of dreams for most of us, evaporating with the morning dew like any other dream. Eventually it begins to sink in that the future and the recent present are behind us, and that we are now witnessing history become the yet-to-come. Diaries, journals, newspapers take on a very different meaning these days as ironic future relics.

With our memories only reaching two months into the old future, and fewer and fewer memories of our *old past/new future,* we are stuck with surprisingly short records of experience. The past no longer remembered, we begin to repeat most of the things we did the day before.

At first, it was just those little specks of details that seemed to be missing or out of place. Like, no longer being able to say with accuracy whether you had steak, broccoli and rice for dinner last night. So you have a strong, almost obsessive feeling that you should have steak, broccoli and rice for dinner again tonight. And you do, because you just can't help yourself.

Or that thing you thought you asked your friend to do yesterday, and they never did it, and you ask them again today. But it turns out you never asked, according to them, and now you kinda can't remember *ever* having asked, either.

But the smaller details are the stitches in the fabric of the bigger details. As the smaller changes build up, the bigger ones become visible. Increasingly, larger scale events are beginning to repeat themselves. And that's the thing. It's still too early to tell if you can meaningfully change something about the past-future and have a different future-past outcome, or if you're just stuck reliving it.

Most people report feeling mechanically compelled to repeat their actions from the previous day (now tomorrow).

Modern language, based on a uni-directional way of living and communicating in the world, will essentially need to be rewritten, now that tense is all confused. Those certain African, Native American, and Asian communities, whose languages depended on a more cyclical notion of time, or whose notions of time incorporate agricultural, astronomical, genealogical, ecological, and economic cycles into its expression, are said to be doing better with the shift than in the countries where Anglo-Saxon culture and linear modes of time dominate, such as here in the U.S.

"For us," said U.N. Kenyan Ambassador Mbasi at a televised conference, "time is only meaningful at the point of the event. It does not becoming meaningful by the clock symbol time, some Western mathematical point."

Children under the age of five, who have different notions of memory to begin with, since they haven't yet been indoctrinated with routines, clocks, and schedules, also seem to be experiencing *The Shift* noticeably different than the rest of us. It seems that our *childhood amnesia*— the inability to recall any episodic memories before the age of three or four —may be some useful defense mechanism after all.

Fortunately, most mechanical memory actions, such as driving and walking, seem to be embedded into our muscles and untouched by the flux in time. But as time continues its slow crawl backward, unraveling, even those motor memories may become unraveled with it.

To the layperson, as explained by your local newscaster or celebrity talk show scientist, the arrow of time has reversed. We are now moving from chaos to order. The universe is shrinking, the Earth is hurdling back into the shadow of an already-traveled path. . .

You get news like this, you quickly start trying to figure out how many seconds you've lived and how many you should have left until. . .well, no one knows what just yet. No one knows what will happen when your own personal timeline's clock reaches zero.

There are a multitude of countdown timer apps to download for every kind of phone. But a few tweaks to your standard kitchen timer will do the trick, too.

The pundits gossip about how soon the world governments will be forced to coordinate and make some official changes to time zones, clocks, calendars, and the like. Those who need to keep track of these things for business purposes have taken to using *Time one* and *Time two.*

Under *Time one, the old time,* today was November seventh, tomorrow was November eighth, and yesterday was November sixth. Under *Time two, the new time,* today is November seventh, yesterday was November eighth, and tomorrow will be November sixth, 2013.

Again.

Everyone has their speculations about what is causing *The Shift*. Blogs the world over, theorize on everything from military experiments gone awry, to the true meaning of the Mayan Calendar's end. Since the shift is estimated to have begun on around January 1, 2014, there are those who purport a connection to the New Year, some sort of reset button had been triggered during the Y2k scare.

One popular theory among the age twenty to twenty-five crowd is that time has simply exploded. Some cult physicists have posited that the rate of information change has increased so rapidly that the human brain, in its current modern design, simply cannot process new information, and is looping back on all of the information it had about the world.

A theory recently released by a well-respected Harvard scientific research team at a news conference, states that the speed of light is decreasing and has been over the centuries. Their research, which they had been conducting years before *The Shift,* demonstrated that the thermodynamic arrow of time was never actually constant.

"The observed uni-directionality of time processes has always been in sharp conflict with the fact that Newton's laws and Einstein's equations work equally well in either time direction," the lead researcher, Dr. Johnny Sing, said when interviewed.

"We think that with the speed of light slowing to a critical speed below its limiting speed, which is the limiting speed for all matter, it appears to have actually, well. . .halted, flipped, and reversed the structure of time, as we know and experience it. We can only perceive the outside world with the assistance of light, which is why nothing can exceed the rate at which we perceive it. With the speed of light lowered, our perception of event order is adjusting with it. "

Reporters asked Sing: why the changes in cause and effect were so subtle? Why *The Shift* seemed only to be having a visible impact on adult human memory? Why, for example, broken eggs were not forming themselves back into full-shelled eggs; or why water did not now run back into the tap?

Dr. Sing simply shrugged and responded, "Now right backwards talking, I am?"

"What?" one reporter asked, high-pitched and sarcastic from the galley of reporters perched outside his office. Other reporters had looks on their faces ranging from confusion to amusement.

Dr. Sing nodded at their reactions, expecting them. "Reporters. I said: 'am I talking backwards, right now?' You people need to get it out of your mind that cause and effect is some mechanical, clockwork, formulaic thing. An origin cause and resulting effect could not be easily or neatly isolated for any event— even before *The Shift* happened. At the quantum scale, classical causality breaks down."

The curious reporter's expression contorted into jester's mask. Unsure of what question to ask next, she only smiled.

Dismissing her with a hand shooing, Dr. Sing took it upon himself to turn and speak directly into the camera. "Listen people: human perception, expectation, and experience are far more powerful and responsible for shaping the physical world than we give them credit for. I suspect that soon, once this thing settles in and the brain does its work to adapt, we will all start to experience the world even more strangely."

All sorts of "treatments" and fixes for the new amnesia are being peddled: memory balms, re-memory creams, and past pills; new meditation and prayer programs, prolonged hypnotic regression sessions are all selling at top dollar to celebrities. If you were bothered by excessive camera phone usage and selfies before, you are increasingly finding it necessary to document more moments of your life in order to remember the new past. But even these moments began to stack up and eventually become useless as we begin to lose hope that we will ever see what we knew as the future again. The dim hum of fear and anxiety that we carry grows louder with each backward day that passes, without a global cure or definitive cause of *The Shift*.

And there will be no finding of *The Shift's* definitive cause yet. There may be no global cure.

Because what they do not yet know, and what I cannot yet reveal, is that I think I may entirely be the cause of *The Shift*. Me and me alone.

I am the accidental Goddess of this universe, where the time order has been reversed. And I do not yet know how to fix it, or— if I am being perfectly honest— whether I *can* fix it.

All I know is that it is imperative that I write this all down, before I lose my memory of it too. I'm going to start at the beginning of when time looped back in on itself. . .

Although, perhaps by now, I should call it the ending.

My name is Afina Newton, and I am a third year PhD candidate in Parallel University's Department of Physics, with a specialization in Quantum Mechanics and Quantum Field Theory.

When you start poking and prodding at the nature of reality, you're liable to get some strange results.

ZERO POINT

(You)

*"Within the void called Time and Space, there
are those who move from reality to reality
creating the programs in which souls experience.
They move through the place known as Zero
Point, where matter and antimatter merge to
create new realities. It is the place where positive
and negative collide to destroy matter and
recreate new. . .it is the home of the creational
forces, those who bend and shape realities
through sound, light, and color. . .closing and
opening, rips in time, movement through space
time. . ."*
—Graham Hancock

You are almost ready to go back out into the world,
Creator. But first, You must visit the Electromagnetic Field to
choose your next experience. You walk down to the Field
which appears infinitely vast. Situated in what seems to be
the Field's center is a large circle with seven computer
terminals mounted around its ring. In the center of the ring
sits a golden chair with living vines crawling on its arms,
star-suns beset in its back.

As You take a seat in the chair, the screens at the
terminals around the circle blink on simultaneously. The
screens projects 3-D holographic images of dodecahedrons,
cubes, pyramids, various pieces of clockwork, and planetary
spheres. The objects appear to be dancing atop the screen as
they contort and flex into different shapes.

A soft, spectral feminine voice speaks out,
dimensionless and heard from every direction:

"Welcome to the Formation Field at Zero Point,
Creator. You do not need to speak aloud or touch the screens.
The Electromagnetic Field and the quantum omniscient bio-
computer terminals pick up directly on Your waves as You
signal them. Although You appear to have a physical body in
the Field, please remember that the appearance is only a
holographic image, bought about by special conditions of the
Field and light reflection off of the biocomputers."

"You only need to *think* in order to communicate with anything around You, so there is no need to 'touch' anything. You will need to choose Your alignments and coordinates carefully for Your next experience. Some factors to consider are: What lessons would You like to learn during Your next experience? What do You hope *to* accomplish?"

A large overhead monitor opens up into a window that looks out into the physical three-D Universe. Using the control panels located beneath each terminal, You can switch the view of the monitor to see a different part of the universe from all possible angles, or to close up on a particular celestial object. You adjust the screen's focal point to the Milky Way galaxy.

The Milky Way comes into view, and You continue to zoom in until You reach the solar system that contains the cluster of nine planets that revolve around the star-sun. This particular cosmos is intertwined with the human experience. The nine planets, their moons, meteors, and other celestial bodies, are sprinkled about the monitor, orbiting elliptically from their respective positions around the solar nucleus.

The sun burns regally, fusing its elements together to emit waves of heat and gas that transform into a glowing, flashing reddish-orange bulb on the monitor.

The voice floods the circle again. "You have chosen to return to planet Earth as the arena for Your next experience. The grid for Earth consists of three dimensions, time, space, and depth mapped upon an electro-magnetic Field. The grid is under the influences of gravity, relativism and self-consistency."

"In the grid You will be conditioned by those rules, although not bound to them. It is incumbent upon You to discover Your own abilities and limitations during Your journey, in accordance with the life patterns You create for Yourself."

You begin entering data into the control panel, charting out planetary positions for Your experience. The large monitor begins to move and steer the planets into positions based upon the information You provide. The sun moves and You set the time and coordinates of re/birth, down to the very moment. Each time-slice fits together piece by piece, forming a concentric circle at their convergent point. You sketch for nearly an Infinity.

"Now, You must create a framework of life events, Creator. Map the events on the space line that is parallel to the timeline of Earth. Remember that You are an architect of Your life experiences."

"There are options for Your re-entry into the Human Experience grid, Creator. Please signal if You would like more detailed information on each option."

You signal affirmatively.

"The **Amenta Program** allows You to enter into a younger body vessel, at the exact time-slice that the vessel enters its 7th year. Using the coordinates and timeline that You have locked in, the (re)birth date of Your new body vessel is March 21, 1986 at 12:01 AM in Philadelphia, PA at Lat 39.57 Long 75.10, " the guide voice explains.

"The **Akhet Program** allows for the rebirth to take place in a body vessel preparing to leave Earth. The Creator currently animating this vessel has chosen an event and a moment in its timeline where it wants to leave the body. This particular Creator's chosen time-slice of death for Its body vessel, is a time-slice that matches closest to Your chosen coordinates for rebirth; within .0000001 of an Earth second; within the same degree of longitude and latitude.

If You pick **Akhet** Program, You will enter the body at that time-slice, the old Creator will be leaving the body vessel as You step into it," the guide voice says.

"The reanimation of the body will occur on July 14, 2013, at 5:15 PM in Philadelphia, PA. You will endow the vessel with a renewed sense of life and spirit. The path that You have chosen during this life planning session will be superimposed upon the destiny of the reanimated body. You will have an opportunity to review this body's life prior to the reanimation during a brief memory assimilation session that will occur as a 'flash' before the eyes.

Please keep in mind You will not yet be firmly threaded into the Earth timeline at that point and can easily produce fluctuations in the vessel's event and timeline. Please allow the assimilation of memory occur without interfering, risking shifts in cause and effect, " the guide voice says.

"Upon execution of Your program, as You re-enter the Earth grid, what You have done here will slowly fade from memory. But what You have done here You will know deep within, for You will be endowed with the ability to sense and know higher truth. The Human Experience is the journey by which You will slowly rediscover those truths, intentions, and lessons that You wish to learn, through the unfolding of Your chosen life line." The guide voice blinks out.

You think about what lesson You want to learn during this version of the Human Experience. You build Your existence step by step, sewing together each time-slice, allowing each one to flow seamlessly into the next. You endow Your existence with intentions, goals, and purpose.

You review the whole of the life in a blink of light. With Your intended path in mind, You choose a program. It begins to download.

You self-actualize. . .

If You choose the AMENTA Program, turn to page 20 and read forward.

If You choose the AKHET Program, turn to page 200 and read backward.

Jaden wiped tears from his face after he pulled the helmet off. He was visibly shaken—nearly hyperventilating. Dr. Zack, a young white guy wearing a white lab coat, was sitting in a chair across from the video game machine. He finished making notes in his pad before throwing Jaden a towel.

"Heeeyy, you came out early! How ya feelin' buddy? You got so many points in that last round! You got rid of two enemy thugs."

"Yeah, I know but I don't really like the way it made me feel! My heart is racing too fast! It feels like I really killed that dude!"

Dr. Zack chuckled. "Jaden, don't worry! That's just an adrenaline rush, little homie. The game is *supposed* to feel real. Imagine how much your friends would love it."

"And plus my mom don't let me play these kinda games at home. She wouldn't like it."

"We won't tell her about this either, if you don't. Remember our little promise?" Jaden shrugged.

The doctor sensed his hesitation. "Besides, your mom knows you're testing out these games for us, buddy. She won't be mad. She's proud of you. You're a software tester! That's big stuff, young man. Plus, we're paying her and you don't wanna mess up that for your mom, right?"

"Okay, I guess so," Jaden said, still hesitant. He knew he wasn't supposed to keep anything from his mother; but what Dr. Zack said seemed right. His mom knew he was there.

"So, ya ready for round two or what?"

"Yeah." Jaden put the helmet back on his head. . .

He gave up his fight and succumbed to the tug. There was a buzzing tingle, then pop! *as his energy was plucked from his physical body. He felt himself being sucked into the vacuum of dark matter settling in around him. Encountering no resistance inside the vacuum, he traveled at light speed.*

There was a tugging sensation. He concentrated all of his consciousness on that black. As the last bullet burrowed into his chest, the images of the world around him dimmed. The streetlights, the restaurant, the row-homes, slowly drained from his eyes and were replaced by a black liquidity...

Thwack-thwack boom!

He collapsed to his knees.

The next bullet hit his right shoulder.

Thwack-thwack boom!

Raheim became momentarily airborne and he felt himself careening through space. Just as suddenly, the gravity switch turned back on, time sped back up, and he was sent back down to the ground, back to the sidewalk.

Thwack, thwack!

The world ceased its spin after the veins in his arms exploded.

The tip pierced through Raheim's skin.

The bullet whistled through the air until it came upon its target. Time crept slowly to a standstill...

Raheim saw the flash of light ignite the air before he heard the sound crack like a leather whip against the silent summer night. "No—wait!"

"Its time for you to join your brother in the cemetery, motherfucker!" the figure called out from beneath his hood, sounding almost unsure of himself.

The hooded figure was clutching something in his left hand,that glinted dully in the glow of the street lights.

Raheim and Khalid stepped into the doorway. Neither of them noticed a Shadow of Death waiting outside, in front of the door. Nor the figure, small and hooded, that stepped out of the shadow to receive them.

"Alright. We'll let those motherfuckas see the sun rise one last time," Khalid spoke with slurred reassurance.

"Look at you man, you're fucked up. Let's let 'em live tonight. It's ten after, cuz. Let's just go home, so you can go to bed, man. We'll ride out tomorrow," Raheim begged.

Khalid snatched his food up from the counter and turned to face Raheim.

"Yeah, let's go find these bitch niggas, man. What time is it, Raheim? I need to get to the crib and get my heat. I know where one they all stay at, too. Right up Blumberg Projects. Let's ride on 'em." Khalid stumbled up to the counter and threw a few crumpled up bills at the woman.

"Yo, Khalid, let's just roll, dude— *please*. Just grab your food." Raheim said.

"We don't want you in store right now! We are closing soon! Take your food and go!" the woman behind the counter screeched at them.

Making a pretend gun with his fingers, Khalid aimed at her head and pulled the trigger.

"Shut up, bitch! I'll murk you too. Gimme my shrimp fried rice."

"Your food is done now! Pay *now!*" she repeated.

Raheim had once read somewhere that the black man is guilty because he's black, and he's black because he's guilty. To some, that's a truth. He shook his head and laughed sadly at Khalid. Raheim stuck out his arm again to steady him.

"I'm trying to calm you down, man! You are fucked up! Take a seat! Chill, Raheim!"

Stop grabbin' on me, nigga!" Raheim reached out to grip Khalid to pull him away from the counter. But he snatched his arm away, losing his balance and falling up against it the window.

The woman standing behind it jumped back, startled. Khalid went up to the counter and banged his fist on the bulletproof glass window that was meant to keep employees safe from unruly customers. Customers like him.

"You see how they treat us? We're just a bunch of niggas to them, we're all suspicious, violent niggers. Check it, cuz I'm a Black man in America, right? You know what that means! They don't give a fuck about me, so why do I care about them? But see, it's fucked up cuz America created niggers, right? They made us, then they hate what they created! Right!?"

"Food is done now. Pay *now!*"

"They murdered my heart, so now I'm gonna murda them. That's the American way, that's the way we take revenge. Fuck that shit, son. This ain't no fucking grief talking, either. And let them come for me! I'm ready for death! I never been afraid to die! I was born to die, ha ha!" Khalid laughed with a near-maniacal glee.

Just pain and death everywhere they turned. There was no higher truth. He looked at the slip of paper again, and scoffed at it before balling it up and flicking it to the dirty floor of the restaurant. Truth.

"Nah, you don't feel that way, dude. That's your grief talking. I'm hurt too, man; but we just have to try to maintain. Taking another life isn't going to bring him back."

Raheim swallowed hard, not knowing if he believed his own words. The sharp, crunchy shards of the fortune cookie scraped at his throat as he listened to Khalid air out his pain.

Khalid walked over to the wall and slumped up against it. His features were twisted into a Halloween mask of grief with tear-streaked cheeks. "I feel like I wanna die right now, cuz, word up. Fuck the world," he said. "I'll kill any fuckin' body right now, moms, granddads, uncles, nieces, cousins, fuckin' babies, dog! I don't give a fuck right now! They killed my little brother! They took my heart. I'm taking out all of their families."

Raheim munched thoughtfully on his fortune cookie for a moment as he considered each word of the fortune individually:

You have an ability to sense and know higher truth.

Raheim tore off the plastic, cracked it, and pulled out the white slip of paper, popping the cookie in his mouth.

Raheim snatched a fortune cookie out of the basket of cookies near the door, as he and his cousin Khalid walked into the Chinese store to pick up their order.

> *"It is a peculiar sensation, this double-consciousness...one ever feels his twoness. . ..two warring souls, two thoughts, two unreconciled strivings; two warring ideals in one dark body, whose dogged strength alone keeps it from being torn asunder."*
> —W.E.B. Du Bois

(Jaden)

AKHET PROGRAM

.sdrawkcab daeR

Akhet Program

APPPENDIX

"Our archives are treasure troves - a testament to many lives lived and the complexity of the way we move forward. They contain clues to the real concerns of day-to-day life that bring the past alive."

—— Sara Sheridan

APPENDIX A

Mechanisms of Psychological, Therapeutic, and Neuro-
biological Research with the PsychoTemporal Transcranial
Stimulation Device

Parallel University
Spring 2002
Dr. Diop Hammond, Black Cultural Studies and Psychology
Depts.
Dr. Noah Miller, Neurology Dept.

Abstract

Combining two notable brain stimulation techniques of
transcranial direct current stimulation (tDCS) and
transcranial magnetic stimulation (TMS), the psychotemporal
transcranial stimulation device (PTSD) uses a noninvasive
method to stimulate several targeted brain regions
responsible for memory and time perception. The PTSD
utilizes an electric coil set in place above the targeted region
of the scalp with rapidly changing magnetic fields to induce
small electrical currents in the brain; simultaneously, a
constant, low current is delivered directly to the targeted
brain areas via small dermal electrodes. This causes either
depolarization or hyperpolarization in the neurons of the
brain; or, on simpler terms, causes excitement or inhibits the
brain. For example, stimulation in the brain area of the
hypothalamus can activate "the sympathetic system control
centers of the heart strongly enough to increase the arterial
blood pressure by more than 100 percent," while other
centers "can control body temperature," "increase or decrease
salivation" and "cause bladder emptying."[32]

---

[32] Rossi, Ernest Lawrence. The Psychobiology of Mind-body Healing: New
Concepts of Therapeutic Hypnosis. New York: W.W. Norton, 1986. Print.

The PTSD targets regions of the brain responsible for short term and long term perceptions of time and memory; specifically, the PTSD stimulates the cerebral cortex, cerebellum, occipital, parietal[33], and frontal lobes, hypothalamus[34], and the basal ganglia. Studies and experiments have conclusively shown that synapses fired in these areas are fired during thought of an action are fired in the same areas as when an action occurs (i.e. taking a walk in the park and imagining taking a walk in the park have similar neural firing patterns). Laboratory research has also demonstrated that "brain function is active, not passive, in its interactions with environment and elucidating the processes operative in this active aspect of mind" and that "the intrinsic cortex and limbic formations of the forebrain actively organize sensory input."[35]

When we think about something that has happened in the past, present or future, different regions of the brain are activated when subjects thought about the past and the future as compared with the present. Mounting neuroscientific evidence also shows that our conscious intentions are closely linked to oscillations of the electromagnetic field at many well-separated brain sites.[36] The PTSD can be used to either disrupt or facilitate brain activity.

---

[33]The prefrontal, medial temporal, and parietal regions show similar increases in activity relative to task control, when imagining the future or recollecting the past. (Okuda et al.,)

[34]The hypothalamus...integrates the sensory-perceptual, emotional, and cognitive functions of mind with the biology of the body. Since the limbic-hypothalamic system is in a process of constantly shifting psycho-neuro-physiological states, all learning associated with it is, of necessity, state-dependent." (Rossi, p.101) "There may well be two kinds of aging clock, one in the brain's hypothalamus orchestrating growth and development, another in each individual cell, the two clocks roughly synchronized and providing what is designed to be a fail-safe system." (Walford, 1983, pp.89-92). Aging is a psychobiological process that has little to do with calendar-year age. Pribam, Karl H., Languages of the Brain: Experimental Paradoxes and Principles in Neuropsychology
[36]H.P. Stapp, A Model of the Quantum Classical and Mind-Brain Connections, and of the Role The Quantum Zeno Effect in the Physical Implementation of Conscious Intent

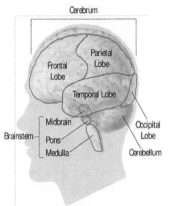
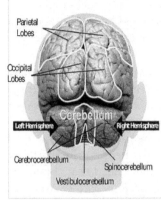

Uses

The two brain stimulation techniques from which the PTSD is adapted (tDCS and TMS) were originally developed for clinical uses such as rehabilitation of stroke patients, Parkinson's disease, fibromyalgia, and post-stroke motor deficits. The techniques were later discovered to have significant psychological and even physical impacts on otherwise healthy adults, leading to improvement in problem solving ability, attention span, memory, movement, and coordination.

While the inventor of the PTSD acknowledges the device's potential to be used in a range of treatments because of its combined use of the two techniques, the PTSD was developed specifically for the purposes observing the effects of electromagnetic brain stimulation on working memory, cognitive tasks, facilitating motor memory formation, enhanced motor performance and motor learning in both healthy volunteers and volunteers suffering from various forms of memory loss, post-traumatic stress disorder, and anxiety disorder. Beyond the expansion, facilitation, excitation, and creation of memories, we have also demonstrated the function of the PTSD during sleep to induce particular dreams.

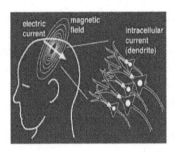

Theoretical Background

Theories of epigentics suggest that particular genetic traits may pass down trans-generationally. These traits, depending on certain triggers in an environment, can switch on or off, catalyzing certain behaviors in a micro-system (such as a cell) or a macro-system (a person's behavioral traits). In much the same way that DNA is encoded in us, it is posited that we also inherent our ancestral memories; when ancestral memory is triggered in an individual, the memories may directly impact upon their health, psychology, or behavior. For example, the psychological disorder known as 'Post-traumatic Slavery Disorder" theorizes that the repeated trauma experienced by people of African descent during slavery and the decades of oppression following it, have passed from generation to generation, resulting in the dysfunctional, self-destructive behaviors patterns that can be witnessed in Black cultures around the world.

Experimental evidence provides insights into this phenomenon; a Duke University group experimented with mice. When female mice were given a diet rich in methyl groups, the fur pigments of their offspring was permanently altered, with the changes to the methyl groups being inherited as a mutation in a gene would be inherited. If diets and chemicals can be inherited, this provides support for the notion that other phenomenon, such as disease, drug abuse, child neglect, can encode changes to the DNA, and passing down from generation to generation.

Recent studies and data in psychology provides further evidence for the passing down of experiences and memories. The social function of memory underlies all of our storytelling, history-making narrative activities, and ultimately all of our accumulated knowledge systems.
Sharing memories with other people performs a significant social –cultural function, the acquisition of which means that the child can enter into the social and cultural history of the family and community.[37]

There are three memory types that the PTSD focused on in therapeutic and experimental use:

1. **episodic memory**—(episode) referring to something that happened once at a specific time and place; i.e. what I had for dinner last night

2. **autobiographical memory**—i.e. the first time you ever saw a film in the theater.

3. **generic memory**—memories that fit recurrent situations, calling for an scripted memory system

According to some hypotheses, "remembering past events and imagining or simulating future events draw on similar kinds of information in episodic memory and involve many shared processes. In particular, episodic remembering and future thinking both depend critically on relational proceses that link or bind together distinct elements of an experience."[38]

---

[37] Nelson, Katherine. "The Psychological And Social Origins Of Autobiographical Memory." Psychological Science 4.1 (1993): 7-14. Print.

[38] Daniel L. Schacter and Donna Ross Addis, On the Constructive Episodic Simulation of Past and Future Event, in Behavioral and Brain Sciences (200_)

Tangential to our studies (but a seemingly natural consequence), we have been able to gather enough data to provide additional evidential support for the phenomenon of "childhood amnesia." The term childhood amnesia Using the PTSD, we were able to stimulate memory recall to gain memories from those periods, where previously participants had drawn blanks.

Childhood amnesia is the inability of adults and adolescents to recall episodic memories before the age of 2–4 years, and also the period around the age of 10, where adults retain fewer memories than might otherwise be expected given the passage of time.[39] However, this is known to vary across gender, culture, with implications in the development of language, and changes in encoding, storage and retrieval of memories during early childhood.[40] Childhood amnesia should also be closely considered in connection to false memories and the development of the brain in early childhood. Katherine Nelson states that "the term childhood amnesia implies that something was there and is lost. This in turn implies that we need to find an explanation either in terms of loss or in terms of some force that interferes with retrieval of memories that still exist."[41]

[39]Robinson-Riegler; Robinson-Riegler, Bridget; Gregory (201_). *Cognitive Psychology: Applying the Science of the Mind* (Third ed.). 75 Arlington Street, Suite 300, Boston, MA: Pearson Education Inc. as Allyn & Bacon. pp. 272–276; 295–296; 339–346.

[40]Hayne, H (200_). "Infant memory development: Implications for childhood amnesia." *Developmental Review* (24): 33–73.

[41]*The Psychological and Social Origins of Autobiographical Memory* by Katherine Nelson, *Psychological Science*, Volume 4, No. 1, January 1993

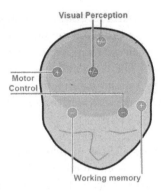

Visual Perception

Motor Control

Working memory

Applied Research Study Details

Parallel U.'s Black Cultural Studies research department launched a longitudinal study on Black cultural memory and its effect on autobiographical memory, using the PTSD and a series of research interviews to elicit data on the ways in which personal memory, collective memory, and cultural history intersected to influence self-identity for modern-day Black Americans. The study also sought to help establish another phenomenon, known as post traumatic slave syndrome, as a clinical diagnosis.

The study, begun in 1994 and ending in 2001, involved multiple in-depth interviews and exposure to the PTSD with 157 African-Americans living in Philadelphia, with the participants ranging in age, gender, and economic background. As part of the interview, participants had to reconstruct personal memories and recall historical events of cultural significance that occurred in their lifetime or prior to their birth.

The study also made use of home video, firsthand accounts in personal journals, and additional interviews with family members of participants to confirm the reconstructed narratives given by participants. Part of the research was an attempt to find a positive nexus or feedback loop between self-identity and cultural memory.

The study involved 4 in-depth interviews with each participant, approximately 60 to 90 minutes in length during which the researcher asked open-ended interview questions regarding the participant's personal experiences and personal histories, and their connection to larger cultural experiences and social histories. These interviews were audio recorded and transcribed. 2 of the interviews were recorded after sessions in the PTSD.

To protect privacy, records of the participants were kept under a code number rather than by name and in locked files. Participants were split into two groups, one which studied past memories, history, and traumatic events, and one that studied memories, current events, and imagined future events, both personal, communal, and global.

There were some risks associated with the study, (see Sections below); However, the study also provided tremendous benefits to participants, including an opportunity to examine one's own experience and history through in depth interviews, and improved self-understanding of one's lived experiences and relationships.

The benefits of the study to the field of sociology, health, education, psychology, culture studies, and more are innumerous. Some benefits including theoretical contributions in the conceptualization of post-traumatic slavery disorder, post traumatic stress disorder, cultural definitions and intersection of class and race, and the significant role time plays in all of these experiences. In addition, one of our research subjects brain evidenced maximal efficiency in communicating information between brain regions, particularly the temporal and frontal cortex areas. The subjects' extraordinary memory recall was instrumental in targeting areas of the brain responsible for memory recall.

Parts and Functions of the PTSD

Parts

- Monitor situated directly before the patient for video input

- 19 EEG channels plus 4 references positioning for accurate spatial resolution

- Gyroscope generating positional information for cursor and camera controls

- Electrodes - two electrodes that deliver constant current. Each device has an anodal electrode and a cathodal electrode.

- Coil – an electric coil built into a helmet is situated just above the scalp and uses electromagnetic induction to generate an electric current across the scalp without physical contact. A plastic-enclosed coil of wire is held next to the skull and when activated, produces a magnetic field oriented orthogonally to the plane of the coil.

- The PTSD uses the signals measured by the coil and electrodes to interpret player facial expressions in real-time. When the participant smiles, the in-console avatar mimics the expression even before the participant is aware of their own feelings, responding just as naturally as the participant would in real time

- The PTSD monitors the participant's emotional states and state of mind in real-time, allowing real-time feedback on participant response, focus, fatigue, and other mental states.

- The PTSD reads and interprets the participant's conscious thoughts and intent, allowing participant's manipulate virtual objects using only the power of thought.

- Certain pulses and frequencies cause neurons in the neocortex under the site of stimulation to depolarize and discharge action potential, and, when used in the primary motor cortex, produces muscle activity

- In some areas of the cortex, the subject will not consciously experience an effect, but his behavior may be slightly altered or changes in brain activity may be detected

- Repetitive stimulation produces longer-lasting effects which persist past the initial period of stimulation. The mechanism of these effects is not clear although it is widely believed to reflect changes in synaptic efficacy akin to long term depression

- There is no strict limitation on the duration of stimulation set at this point but a stimulation time of 20 minutes is considered the ideal time. The longer the stimulation duration, the longer the observed effects of the stimulation persist once the stimulation has ended. A stimulation length of 10 minutes results in observed effects lasting for up to an hour. It is generally encouraged to wait at least 48 hours to a week before repeating the stimulation.

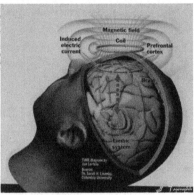

Risks and Side Effects

There are a few minor side effects that can be felt by the patient while receiving the stimulation, and most of these can be controlled by correct set up of the device. Side effects may include skin irritation, a phosphene at the start of stimulation, nausea, headache, fainting, minor cognitive changes, dizziness, itching under the electrode, and on rare occasions, seizures, minor cognitive changes and psychiatric symptoms, (particularly a low risk of mania in depressed patients). Though other side effects are thought to be possibly associated with the PTSD, they are considered investigative and lacking substantive proof.

Temporal disorders typically occur when the electrodes are placed above themastoid, which are used for stimulation of the vestibular system. Some patients, while reliving their memories, can distinguish between their current experience and the vivid memories that they were recalling. They stated this felt like having two simultaneous streams of consciousness, with an awareness that they were observing their memories. ramping up the current can reduce this sensation. This is done by slowly increasing the current until the desired current is reached.

The same safety protocols that are used to administer tDCS and TMS are used for the PTSD. Since this technique of stimulation is still being explored, safety precautions should be kept. The set protocols must be followed to ensure correct use of the device. As more is discovered about the use of PTSD, safety standards may evolve, which is why it is critical to remain up to date with the most current safety protocols.

APPENDIX B

Interdepartmental Memo

To: Jack Stone, Branch Chief

From: Samuel Richter, Warden

cc: Dr. Juanita Gerald

Re: Research Study

We are participating in a Research project being conducted by PU, regarding youthful male offenders in an effort to identify early predictors of antisocial behavior. The study requires 132 participants. Eligible participants must be males between the ages of 13 and 17, and must be African-American or Hispanic. Report progress by December 16 to D.H. at PU.

The following names have been selected for study:

Robert Wxxxxxxxx

Nasir Axxxxx

James Jxxxxxx

APPENDIX C[42]

5 major cognitive changes that occur during adolescence:

- Become able to think about what is possible, instead of limiting thought to what is real.

- Better able to think about abstract concepts.

- Begin thinking more about the process of thinking.

- Become able to think in multiple dimensions at once and weigh those dimensions before taking course of action.

- Develop ability to see things in relative, rather than black-and-white, terms.

Characteristics/factors that interfere with "adult-like" thinking:

- *Risk-taking behavior*

- *Present-oriented thinking.*

- *Egocentrism*

- *Perceived invulnerability*

- *Magical or wishful thinking*

- *External factors*

---

[42] Excerpt from Understanding Adolescents: A Juvenile Court Training --- Curriculum - KIDS ARE DIFFERENT: How Knowledge of Adolescent Development Theory Can Aid Decision-Making in Court

(Created by Juvenile Law Center, American Bar Association Juvenile Justice Center, Youth Law Center)

APPENDIX D

Case Study (2000)

One of our research subjects L.K. (fictitious initials used for confidentiality), an African-American female of approximately 14.5 years of age, exhibited extraordinary memory recall. The subject was identified by DHS as a viable candidate for the study. During initial interviews, we were skeptical about L.K.'s abilities and had to search for objective means of evaluating and verify her claims. This proved difficult for several reasons. One reason was due to the subject's age. Adolescents at that age are not yet sufficiently developed at fitting their subjective sense of time/time rate into the objective sense of time that adults are more attuned to. (see also research and studies on child maturation, sense of time, and brain development). Another reason for difficulty in verifying her memories is the fact that the subject is a part of the foster care system and all of her immediate family is deceased. The subject does not have family videos, pictures, or other accounts of a family history by which we can verify her memories. However, we enjoyed access to the subject's medical history, which showed some history of treatment by a psychologist for depression anxiety from age 11, and some interesting notes on a condition known as "paramnesia." This verified that the subject displayed this very interesting ability at a young age.

The subject kept extensive journals which proved of some
assistance, though researchers had to spend considerable
time attempting to verify fact from fiction in the subject's
writings (some of the journal entries from the early ages
used highly metaphorical, fantastical, and abstract language,
as might be expected.). We queried her about some public
events receiving considerable media attention that might
stick out in the mind of an adolescent of similar age,
maturity, and intelligence (though the subject did test higher
than average on the IQ test that we gave to all research
participants). The subject was mostly accurate on these
queries; however, her strongest areas of memory recall
involved personal events, beginning with the date of March
14. The subject's mother committed suicide in their home on
that date, the details of which were verified with the subject's
caseworker. The subject was about age 7 at the time. L.K.
has an automatic memory recall of any date after that
(notably around the age range when childhood amnesia kicks
in for most children). L.K.'s automatic recall was
distinguished by highly organized and readily accessible
memories of most of the days of her life from pre-
adolescence to her current age. These memories are
extremely lucid memories of her past (and future, as the
subject claims), that she is able to attach mental dates to.
L.K.'s memory recall functioned more like a diary, as opposed
to a precise video or audio that has recorded every moment
of her existence. She associated autobiographical and

episodic memory with particular calendar dates, and could recall on that basis.

If we asked the subject to recall a particular memory on a particular date in the past, the subject would sit quietly and gaze off into the distance for a moment before closing her eyes, Then she would open her eyes and, appearing as if hypnotized, began describing the memory of an event in the present tense, as if she were present in the scene. If we asked the subject to recall a particular "memory" on a date in the future, she would fall into a similar state of recall.

One particular entry in the subject's journal was telling of this ability. We were able to copy the entry:

January 20, 1999 – This is the day i first knew that I could see into the future, although it's probably more accurate to say that that's the first time I "remembered" that I could see. 7 year old me, staring deeply into my own eyes in the mirror, looking for my mom there, getting lost in it. My present state of mind for some flash of a moment, was looking at myself in the mirror as a 7 year old. Although my spirit returned to the future (present day), a piece of my consciousness became trapped inside the mind of 7 year old me. Every day I have lived burdened with the memory of the future. I knew what would happen in the future, but still had to live out every moment of it. There are no perks to living in a perpetual state of déjà vu, not when you cant avoid the consequences and feel powerless to change things. My own mother knew that. I now know, looking back, that it was always me, the one in my head. It was always my future self.

The subject did not possess photographic memory, and was unable to recall the minutiae of her daily experiences. For example, she expressed difficulties in remembering to turn her homework in on time, and difficulties with memorizing formulas in mathematics.

The subject said she often had to make lists and write notes to herself in order to remember the small things. As noted above, the subject also keeps a highly detailed journal, which she told researchers helped to keep her "focused in the moment." The subject also exhibited highly detailed dream recall ability, as well as some sleep disturbances, such as night terrors, sleep paralysis, and frequent nightmares. After several extensive interviews and displays of the memory recall ability, we began using magnetic resonance imagining (MRI) scans built into early models of the PTSD, which showed that several brain regions varied in size and shape from the other test subjects. The structure of the fibers in the white matter of her brain evidenced maximal efficiency in communicating information between brain regions, particularly the temporal and frontal cortex areas. Given that all of L.K's immediate family is deceased and she has no other relatives we were able to contact, we could not determine if there was any genetic basis for L.K.'s abilities.

Her extraordinary memory recall was instrumental in targeting areas of the brain responsible for memory recall and she was of great experimental value to the team. The subject expressed a desire to be treated for the ability, and exhibited many signs of trauma and PTSD, which we treated her for.

APPENDIX E

Press Release

Parallel University
Press
Release

A new grant from a new institute dedicated to exploring questions about the foundations of physics and the origin of the universe will help a Parallel University student physicist with her research on gravity, black holes and the creation of the universe.

Afina Newton, PhD candidate in the Physics Department at Parallel U., will use a $125,111 grant from The Future Sciences Institute to complete an interpretation she helped create of a model for quantum gravity.

"I am crafting my own version of a theory that will unify the two branches of theoretical physics—quantum gravity and general relativity -- for a quantum theory of gravity," Newton said. "I hope that this will tell us more about black holes and the nature of gravity. Lots of research in the past 5 years supports the proposition that space, time and even gravity itself may not be fundamental properties or forces, but in fact may be emergent properties within a deeper theory," "My work will seek to identify quantum information theory as the best source for an emergent theory of gravity."

Newton's research and experimentation will be applied to small black holes to see how their formation, radiation and interaction with matter differ from the classical predictions. Interestingly, Newton, who minored in cultural anthropology in undergrad, says she not only finds support for her work in current mainstream quantum field theory research, but also in ancient traditions, art, and mythology pre-dating science itself. "African astro-physical traditions totally anticipate all of these scientific discoveries. You can dig into Egyptian mythology, for example, and find correlations to the electron, plasma, and radio galaxies in the mythical battle of Horus against Set, where Horus loses his eye," Newton said.

Newton wants to take her research one step further: she wants to see how it might be applied for possible time travel in the future. "This information will also be used to study the feasibility of using small artificial black holes as sources of energy for time travel," she said. "While this is not something that will happen in the near-future, I'm happy for the opportunity to explore these possibilities for our future generations."

Newton's grant was part of The Future Sciences Institute's inaugural grant award of $2 million to 40 grant recipients, aimed at increasing the representation of men and women of color in research and experimental sciences.

Source: Parallel University

APPENDIX F

Glossary of Selected Terms and Concepts

Amenta
This symbol represents the Underworld or Land of the Dead. Originally it meant the horizon of the sun set. Later, it became the symbol of the west bank of the Nile, where the sun set and also where the Egyptians traditionally buried their dead (ancient—symbols.com)

Ahket
1: In ancient Egyptian, the place where the sun rises and sets; often translated as "horizon" or "mountain of light
2: The "Akhet season" or inundation season, ran approximately from mid-July to mid-November in Ancient Egypt, and was the first of three seasons of the ancient Egyptian calendar

Arrow of time
Subjective sense of time determined within brain by thermodynamic arrow of time. Disorder increases with time because we measure time in the direction in which disorder increases [circular time justifies itself via definition]

Black hole
A region of spacetime where gravity is strong enough to ben spacetime around so that its pinched off from the rest of the universe. A singularity is the center of the black hole, a mathematical point of zero volume

Bootstrap Paradox
The bootstrap paradox, or ontological paradox, is a paradox of time travel in which information or objects can exist without having been created. After information or an object is sent back in time, it is recovered in the present and becomes the very object or information that was initially brought back in time in the first place (Wikipedia.com)

Causality
The relation between a cause and its effect or between regularly correlated events or phenomena

Episodic Memory
Reconstructs particularities of specific events that have happened to the individual, such as the people involved in the event, the actions that took place, the setting, and the reactions and emotions involved in the event.

Event
1: something that occurs in a certain place during a particular inter val of time.
2: *Physics.* in relativity, an occurrence that is sharply localized at a single point in space and instant oftime. (Dictionary.com)

Frame of reference
1: an arbitrary set of axes with reference to which the position or motion of something is described or physical laws are formulated
2: a set of ideas, conditions, or assumptions that determine how something will be approached, perceived, or understood (Merriam-Webster.com)

Hyperspace
Extension of the idea of 4-dimensional spacetime to more dimensions (4-dimesnional spacetime may be embedded in hyperspace, just as a 2-dimensional sheet of paper is embedded in 3-dimensional space)

Khepri
An Egyptian solar deity representing creation and rebirth, specifically connected with the rising sun and the mythical creation of the world. The name stems from the Egyptian verb *kheper,* meaning to "come into being"

Light cone
The surface describing the temporal evolution of a flash of light in Minkowski spacetime

Photon
A quantum of electromagnetic radiation, a unit of intensity of light at the retina

Poincaire recurrence/recurrence plot (RP)
1: A recurrence is a time the trajectory returns to a location it has visited before. The recurrence plot depicts the collection of pairs of times at which the trajectory is at the same place

2: In mathematics, the Poincaré recurrence theorem states that certain systems will, after a sufficiently long but finite time, return to a state very close to the initial state. The Poincaré recurrence time is the length of time elapsed until the recurrence (this time may vary greatly depending on the exact initial state and required degree of closeness) (Wikipedia.com)

Superluminal
A frame of reference traveling with a speed greater than the speed of light c

Wave function collapse
The reduction of the physical possibilities of a sate into a single possibility as seen by an observer

Zep Tepi
Zep Tei refers to "First Time", a remote epoch prior to ancient Egypt. It is a place of awakening and a place of forgetfulness. It is the beginning and the end of all and everything. It is the home of the creational forces, those who bend and shape realities through sound, light and color. The term Zep, Zipper, closing and opening, rips in time, movement through space time, DNA is a polymer or encoded DNA. Zep Tepi is Genesis. Zep means Time. Tepi means First. Together they are the First Time or the Golden Age of Alchemy where the gods moved through the Void and created the grids of our reality. We know them as the Egyptian Gods highlighted by Osiris who is associated with Orion, god of resurrection and rebirth. (CrystalLinks.com)

Zero Point
Zero-point energy, also called quantum vacuum zero-point energy, is the lowest possible energy that a quantum mechanical physical system may have; it is the energy of its ground state (Wikipedia.com)

Appendix G

Khepri Livingston's Natal Chart Excerpt (via cafeastrology.com)

Zodiac in degrees 0.00			Placidus Orb:0		
Sun	Aries	0.18	Ascendant	Sagittarius	10.20
Moon	Cancer	28.36	II	Capricorn	13.49
Mercury	Pisces	21.55 R	III	Aquarius	22.08
Venus	Aries	15.00	IV	Pisces	28.22
Mars	Sagittarius	26.26	V	Aries	27.31
Jupiter	Pisces	6.46	VI	Taurus	20.37
Saturn	Sagittarius	9.42 R	VII	Gemini	10.20
Uranus	Sagittarius	22.21	VIII	Cancer	13.49
Neptune	Capricorn	5.44	IX	Leo	22.08
Pluto	Scorpio	6.54 R	Midheaven	Virgo	28.22
Lilith	Gemini	2.31	XI	Libra	27.31
Asc node	Taurus	0.14	XII	Scorpio	20.37

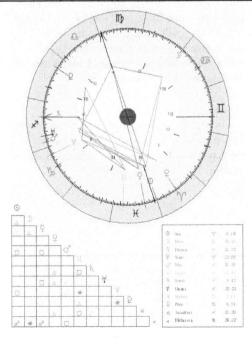

You invest much of your pride and energy into your personal and private life, your home, and your family. Privacy is important to you. You are naturally protective of your family, including your heritage, and of your personal life. Avoid being defensive as you work to build a secure foundation for yourself and the people you love.

You have a desire to be something special or to experience something more than the ordinary. You are a day-dreamer and idealist. It is easy for you to trust others, even (and perhaps especially) people who might seem from the outside looking in as unsavory types. You are looking to identify with something beyond what is normally expected of people. You may have had a childhood that didn't help you direct or define your life. Perhaps the early family life was lacking in supervision or clearly defined rules. A father figure may have been absent or distant and ineffective. Whatever the case may be, you struggle with defining who you are. You might gravitate towards the "wrong people", or get in with the "wrong crowd" in an attempt to define who you are. You might be susceptible to being taken advantage of by others, especially by men or authority figures. You may be easily led astray by peculiar desires or self-destructive habits. You might be attracted to Neptune-ruled behaviors, such as secret affairs, drugs, or other escapist behaviors. There can be some confusion about the past (such as remembering childhood experiences in ways that are far removed from reality), and a tendency to daydream. You may struggle with early conditioning that made you feel tossed aside or neglected in some way, and certainly not directed or supported. You are very sensitive, especially with regards to any real or imagined blows to your ego. You are likely to recognize at some point in your life that you have a tendency to engage in escapist and self-destructive fantasies and/or habits. It is useful to be able to connect these behaviors with their probable source, which is likely to be a weakly-defined ego and identity in childhood.
Often, they are quite wrapped up in themselves. Their memories of the past are outstanding, especially for all things emotional. Moon in Cancer people are never detached--they cling to things, their home, and people they care for. They seek out security and familiarity in all they do. They look for peace and quiet. Their attachment to all that is safe means they are a little leery of change. These peace-loving souls dislike superficiality in all of its forms. They are devoted and accommodating. The insecure ones accumulate things in an attempt to feel secure.

Because of their strong attachment to, and memory of, the past, others may complain that Moon in Cancer natives tend to whip a dead horse. They may dwell on hurts long after everyone else has moved on. When they feel they have been taken for granted (which may be often!), they don't always confront others directly. This is when they can use roundabout ways to get your attention. In fact, these natives, when they are insecure, can become quite manipulative. They can also be victims of habit. These people can have a hard time compartmentalizing their lives, simply because their watery Moon tends to know no boundaries. Sometimes, as a result, they may act irrationally.

Short description:

She is likeable and sociable. Very sensitive to environmental conditions and surroundings. She likes home, habits, comfort and her little world. Very caring and protective of loved ones.

Weaknesses: subject to indolence, inertia. She is impressionable and too sensitive. Family problems.

Moon in VIII

She has a tendency to having deep and profound dreams. Romantic fantasies. Is interested in the occult.

While you have a strong need for emotional security, you are also a person who is drawn to pushing your own limits, and many lifestyle changes can be the result of this need to challenge, or reinvent, yourself emotionally. You are always fascinated with how people work, taboos, secrets, and all that is forbidden or hidden.
This is an especially curious and inquisitive position for Mercury. You are generally very interested in reading, teaching, speaking, exchanging ideas, keeping current with the daily news, and perhaps gossiping. Your interests are many and varied, sometimes to the point that you barely skim the surface of any one topic. You are also very easily distracted and your attention span can be quite short. Quick to learn, you are also swift to share what you know with others. You can be very talkative when you have the chance. You can be a list maker, and often are quite involved in your community. Some of you can be quite nervous or fidgety.

-24 Square Mercury - Mars

While her spirit is lively, it is also cunning. She often acts without thinking, she throws herself into things and exaggerates - and this can bring certain problems. She is nervous and irascible. She can develop others' ideas, while they hesitate - she never does: she presses on.. She cannot stay in the same place, likes change even if it means a backward step in her professional career. She possesses exceptional energy. She is impulsive but bold. She takes on risky enterprises for the good of the community, with all the energy she possesses. She has a great need of her independence, likes her freedom of action.

Her feelings are dominated by wisdom and geared towards the ideal. She likes water, sea voyages. She likes odd people. She suffers professional setbacks because she is too impulsive, imprudent and lacks forethought. She is intuitive, sensitive. Not a fighter and is indecisive. May have some identity problems until she decides on a more spiritual or artistic path. May be psychic or simply strongly intuitive. Gentle and yielding.
Ascendant in Sagittarius

The world is filled with adventure, new things to experience, and, most of all, hope, with this Ascendant. There is an unmistakable faith and enthusiasm with Sagittarius rising people. Grand schemes, big promises, and a willingness to explore and experiment are themes, although follow-through is not a strong characteristic of Sagittarius. These individuals are somewhat restless and often active people. They always seem to be looking for something that is just out of grasp -- and many do this their entire lives. They can be quite direct at times, yet they are likable enough to forgive for their faux-pas. Most have a lot to say and offer. Their insights and opinions are usually interesting and exciting, although sometimes lacking in details.

Sagittarius rising people have opinions about everything, and they just love telling others exactly what they are. Not all people with this position are outgoing folk, but they all have a way of moving about that at least exudes a certain level of confidence. Some might even call them naive or overly optimistic. Even the quiet ones don't shrink from life and from experience. One of the most obvious and endearing traits of Sagittarius rising is their willingness to keep up a sense of humor. Even when they're feeling low, they manage to find humor in life and have fun with whatever they do have. The placement of Sagittarius' ruling planet, Jupiter, will give more clues to how they go about expressing themselves. Jupiter in Capricorn, for example, might give a more sarcastic approach, but underneath there lies an unmistakable hope and spirit for living.

House III in Aquarius

She is always at the forefront of progress. Likes everything that is new, original and ingenious. Likes every new idea, as long as it improves life and naturally is good for everyone. She is happy to travel even at a moment's notice, likes a life full of change and meetings.

House IV is the area of home, family, roots, and deep emotions/sense of self-worth.

House IV in Pisces

She is very susceptible to the mood of those around her. A hard difficult upbringing can mark her for life. When a child, has to be protected, given confidence.

House V is the area of creative self-expression, romance, entertainment, children, and gambling.

RECURRENCE PLOT PT. 2

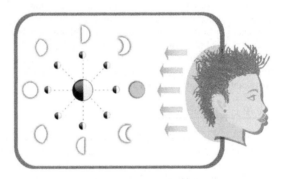

COMING WINTER 2015

Made in United States
North Haven, CT
06 April 2022

17990949R00127